2850

W9-CCO-812

MANN, EDWARD ANDREW   6.95
THE PORTALS

This book belongs to

DATE DUE

Joan R. Skinner
100 N. College
Rensselaer, In
47978

THE PORTALS

Edward Andrew Mann

SIMON AND SCHUSTER
NEW YORK

FOR LORNA AND PAULINE

PROLOGUE

◎

He was a collector of all things, from antiques to books, from objets d'art to paintings, and his manor outside Epernay was a cluttered museum of uncatalogued relics of many years' search. Henri, Baron de Chantille, could not resist the old book, though he did not know the value, nor could he recognize the writing it contained. It might have been valueless or it could have something priceless, but it would probably fall in between, and closer to the former than the latter. He had bought many things in his years of trekking through Syrian bazaars and deserts, poking through piles of junk or excavating for the bits and pieces of archaeology. Partly, it was his work with the Musée Nationale, and partly it was his own unquenchable thirst to collect anything that pulled him away from the empty glittering life of Paris. During the bleak winter months, he had his annual trek to Syria, to continue his work and his hobby. He needed both worlds as man needs both water and air, and could give up neither for the other.

He and Campion, his assistant, had both spent the morning digging through bric-a-brac in the desert bazaar, until they spotted the tiny stall up the side street, one they had not seen before. The old Arab who ran it seemed

7

neither anxious to sell them anything nor worried about the profits he would make. Campion had found an old oil lamp, which he rubbed in jest, saying he expected a puff of smoke from the bottle and a life of ease thereafter. The old Arab took afront.

"Westerners scoff at our ways and our legends, but there is more truth in them than you or I can know."

"I meant no offense," Campion said, sincerely.

"There are many things in this world that we do not know, things which should be left unknown, for they bring great evil."

Campion, not wishing to enter into a debate with the old man, simply agreed. But the old man was not finished. "You do not believe our old tales."

"Well, no," Campion was forced to admit. "I am a scientist."

"Does your science have the answers to the mysteries of life?"

"Not all, no, but when the answers are found, it will be science that finds them." Campion spoke in a friendly and conciliatory manner, yet without compromising his beliefs.

The baron stepped between them. "Men will never understand the mysteries of the Lord."

This seemed to placate the old man. "Ah, here is one who does not scoff. Would you then be interested in a book which holds all the secrets of mankind?"

The baron was not, but wishing to appease the Arab, answered, "I am interested in whatever you have to show."

The old man promptly disappeared through the hanging strings of beads that shielded the doorway and returned with a huge, dusty volume which he set down in front of the baron. De Chantille started to leaf through the pages.

He did not recognize the writing. "Pierre," he said, indicating the book. The younger man came closer and looked. "Do you recognize the language?"

"No, sir."

"It is the writings of the ancient magicians," the old man said. "They say it comes from the Cave of Ali Baba, that once it was possessed by the Old Man of the Mountains, that it is the most ancient of books and that it has the knowledge of the ones who walked the earth before us."

"Where did you get it?" the baron asked.

"A caravan that passed this way some months ago."

"Do you know where it came from?"

"Ah," the old man shrugged, "these things can be passed from caravan to caravan for generations. It could come from those who rob the graves or from another bazaar in a faraway place. One does not have eyes to see. But it is very old."

The baron turned his attention to the book again, feeling the paper and examining the bindings. "I can see that it is. Very old indeed. But you do not know the language in which it is written?"

"The writings of the ancient magicians were only for their eyes. It is not a language that those unschooled in the old arts would know."

Campion and the baron spent a few more minutes examining the book, the strange writing and the even stranger symbols.

"That could be the symbol for Seth," Campion said, pointing to one of the symbols, which appeared something like the image of the Egyptian god.

"Yes, it is similar, but not quite the same." The baron looked up at the old man. "What would you take for this?"

"One thousand French francs, Monsieur."

9

The baron shook his head. "It is a great deal for something which could be worthless." The old Arab shrugged. "Five hundred francs."

"Eight hundred."

And so they bargained for almost an hour before settling on a price of seven hundred francs.

"It is yours," the Arab said, "but take care. The secrets held within those bindings are powerful, if the legends are true. And one should not dabble in them without full knowledge."

"I promise you, I shall take care," the baron said, winking at his assistant so the old man could not see.

"Visit my bazaar again, Monsieur," he said, as the two Frenchmen went out into the harsh sunlight.

"Why did you buy it?"

"It is old. Who knows, it might have some value. But I simply cannot resist an antique book, whatever it is."

"Well, at least it may have a curse to increase the value." Campion laughed.

"Perhaps."

Later, as the coldness of the desert night settled, the baron stood up. He started back toward the camp on the very sands his ancestor had ridden on in the days of the Crusades, and he wondered about the book. There were so many unsolved and inexplicable things in the world that he had a respect for the old knowledge. It would take a great deal of effort, but he decided to translate the book, if he could, when he returned to his home. If there were secrets, he wanted to know them. But he would not mention it to his young associate. Even the self-assured baron did not wish to appear silly in the eyes of his fellow scientists.

CHAPTER ONE

◎

It was a truly magnificent setting: the 18th-century decor and muraled walls, the enormous chandelier which glittered like a thousand diamonds over their heads, the centerpiece of autumn leaves and flowers, and the superb cuisine of an elegant French country house. At one end of the table sat Marcel du Pont, the suave, sophisticated lawyer, and at the other end, his beautiful wife, Marianne, and between them, drinking in the atmosphere, was Cary Ralston.

Ralston idly speculated on the rush of events that had brought him into the countryside outside of Paris instead of flying back to California. Only hours before, he and Du Pont had sat opposite each other at another table while the final legal details of the merger between Electronique Française S.I.F. and California Computer Corporation, Inc. were satisfactorily settled. Du Pont had invited his American counterpart to lunch and it was in the comfortable surroundings of a small restaurant that they discovered a mutual interest in old books. When Du Pont told him of the forthcoming sale of Henri de Chantille's extraordinary collection, Ralston could not resist and had immediately accepted the Frenchman's invitation to visit his home and to attend the auction.

"Tomorrow we shall see some things," Du Pont now said with emphasis and anticipation, putting down his napkin. "Henri's collection was superb."

"I didn't know you knew him," Ralston said.

"I didn't, actually," Du Pont said with a shrug. "Marianne did."

"Only slightly," she said. "Our families knew one another. No one really knew Henri well."

"He was a gentleman archaeologist," Du Pont added. "Always off to some bizarre area like Egypt or Syria and when he returned, he'd just bury himself in that place, cataloging, what have you."

"Yes, he was a scholar. You know how they are . . . *reclus*." She hesitated a moment before going on. "But then some say other things."

"Like what?" Ralston asked.

"There are always these rumors surrounding aristocratic families, especially in the villages. You know how the peasants carry tales," Du Pont replied.

"They say he learned things in the East . . . Black Magic . . ." Marianne said.

"Rubbish," Du Pont muttered.

"Then how do you explain the accident?"

Marcel du Pont shrugged and waved his hand impatiently, as if dusting away the suggestion. "What is there to explain?"

"He was driving alone on the Grand Corniche," Marianne explained to Ralston, ". . . above Nice . . . driving very slowly . . . then suddenly, his car swerved off the road and went into the retaining wall. It burst into flames."

12

"It could have been a heart attack," Du Pont said; Ralston was thinking the same thing.

"And why did the car burst into flames when it was going so slowly?"

"I suppose a gas line could have broken," Ralston offered.

"And finally," she said defiantly, "why are the police so secretive?"

"Ah, so that is it. My wife is upset because her dear friend at the Sûreté will tell her nothing."

"Oh, Marcel, that is not true," she said with a playful pout. "But you know he would tell me unless there was some very good reason not to."

"You should have been a lawyer, my dear." He put his hand on her shoulder affectionately; her fingers moved up to his.

"What do you suspect, Marianne?" Ralston asked.

"I don't know. Nothing really. But with all the talk about the family, one wonders, that's all."

"What kind of talk?"

"Well, for example, they say one of his ancestors was a witch during The Affair of the Poisons and was burned at the stake."

"She was indeed," Du Pont said.

"I'm afraid my history is pretty rusty," Ralston admitted.

"The Affair of the Poisons was during the time of Louis Quatorze. Many, many aristocrats were involved in murders, literally hundreds of cases. It was quite a scandal. The poisons were provided by witches and many court officials were suspected of being involved with Satanic cults. There were confessions, but they were extracted by torture. But as I said before, these stories always surround old families, perhaps because the more history you have, the easier it is to find a black sheep."

"But Marcel, even when Henri was alive, they said strange things roved about his estate at night and sometimes there were horrible shrieks . . ."

"Stories?" Du Pont gestured doubtfully. "Rumors."

"My father believed them. He was a professor of paleontology," Marianne said, turning to Ralston to establish credibility. "In fact, I remember once when I was a little girl my cousins were staying with us. The two boys had gone out riding near Henri's estate. Their horses became badly frightened, wild, and one of the boys was thrown. I remember when they came back to the house, Father warned the boys not to go near there again because there was *something evil* about the place."

"Well, it all makes for a good story, especially when a storm is brewing." Du Pont glanced out the window and up to the sky. "The country house, the storm, and ghost stories. But," Du Pont waved his hand, "we cannot afford storytelling just now. Monsieur Ralston and I must go over the catalogs to see which volumes we will attempt to buy."

"Henri was one of the most diligent collectors in France," Marianne informed Ralston. "It is a pity there are no heirs. I hate to see all his possessions sold."

"When I have a chance such as this, my dear, I feel less sad."

"Some of those things had been in his family for hundreds of years," his wife replied sadly, thinking of her own long ancestry and the accumulations of centuries in her own house.

"For Monsieur Ralston and myself, that will make tomorrow an even more exciting prospect. Now then,

Cary, we must settle ourselves in the library and do some serious thinking."

They left at nine the next morning for the auction. It was still drizzling, but the heavy storm of the night before had passed on. It took them only twenty minutes to reach the Château de Chantille. It was a huge, forbidding stone mansion set on a bleak knoll, surrounded by even bleaker leafless trees, against a background of dark, almost black, soil, quite different from the neighboring countryside.

"Cheery place," Ralston said with a shudder. "You mean to say he lived there all alone?"

"There were servants, of course."

"All hunchbacks, no doubt." Du Pont smiled at Ralston's quip. The closer they got, the more oppressive the place appeared, but the grimness was somewhat dispelled by the cars parked around it; there were several Rolls-Royces, some with English plates, a couple of Mercedes 600s with German plates, and Swiss, Italian, and Austrian registrations on Mercedes, Masseratis, Ferraris, and chauffeur-driven Citroëns. It was a rich crowd.

Du Pont parked his car and they walked across the muddy, gravel driveway toward the house. The château seemed to hover over them, a great dreary hulk, almost ominous against the gray sky. Inside, it proved equally grim. But the well-dressed people milling about filled it and their gay conversation diffused the gloom. The book auction was in the library. Other people went into the drawing room or climbed the stairs to where other objects were being sold.

Everyone in the library carried the same blue-and-white catalog. Ralston thought he recognized a man he'd seen at auctions in New York.

"I'm sure you are quite right," Du Pont said. "I see some familiar faces too." He nodded to several people.

A rather conservative-looking old man with diaphanous skin passed amongst the crowd and took his place on the dais. "Item one, a fine 1847 edition of the *Iliad.*"

And so the bidding began. Du Pont and Ralston both became intent on the sale. The first hundred books were sold within forty minutes. Then a first edition of Voltaire went to a Boston combine for four hundred thousand francs after excited bidding.

When some lesser volumes came under the hammer, Ralston's eyes roved the room and fixed on a portrait hanging above the fireplace. From the subject's modern dress, he assumed it was the late baron. He was a handsome man with silver hair who looked more Nordic than French, but there was something in the eyes which attracted Ralston's interest—a deep fear, as if the man had just looked on the face of the Medusa.

The announcement of a volume in which Du Pont had exhibited some interest the night before broke Ralston's concentration on the portrait. He located Du Pont on the other side of the room and saw him nod ever so imperceptibly. Then again. When the hammer went down, there was not the slightest trace of emotion on Du Pont's face to indicate whether he'd succeeded or not.

Shortly after lunch, Ralston got a set of Alexandre Dumas lesser works for six thousand dollars and was very pleased with himself. He was sure the set could be sold in the States for double that amount and it was a good deal less than his top estimate. His spirits soared and, having tasted blood, he was swept up in the adventure like a gambler who has won. He bought a limited edition of T. E. Lawrence, and an original Zola. By four o'clock, he'd spent over twenty thousand dollars. But the value of his purchases in the States would far exceed that. To a knowledgeable collector, these were investments, rare items which could only appreciate in value as time went on. After four, many of the bidders started to leave, the better volumes having been sold. Only a scattering of people were left when the auctioneer announced lot 604, a case of uncataloged books. There were five such cases, the last items of the day. The bidding was lackluster and the case went for under a thousand dollars.

"Lot 605, a case of uncataloged books," the auctioneer said. Without quite knowing why, Ralston decided to bid. He got it for eleven hundred dollars and the following item, lot 606, another case of books, for nine hundred. He wasn't really sure why he'd done it, except a hope that somewhere in the cases would be a "find." It was like the age-old dream of buying an ordinary painting only to later find you'd purchased a Rembrandt.

"You are a gambler," Du Pont said, as they headed for the car.

"How many books do you reckon those cases would hold?"

Du Pont thought a moment. "Two or three hundred."

"That's what I thought. Well, those are decent odds, 200–1. Thank you very much for clearing my checks with them."

"Nothing."

"I appreciate it. In fact, I cannot thank you enough for mentioning this auction. I've done better than I expected."

"Then I am satisfied."

The next morning, Du Pont and Marianne insisted on driving Ralston to Orly Airport. Shortly after noon, the Pan American 747 lifted off and headed across the Pole to California.

CHAPTER TWO

◎

When the plane was only fifteen minutes from touch-down at L.A. International, Ralston took off the flight slippers and put on his shoes. He settled back in the first-class seat and glanced out the starboard window. The sky was changing to an awesome vermilion along the Califor-nia coastline. He was tired after the twelve-hour flight, but the sight of home revitalized him. As the sky became crimson, the plane turned in across the city and the lights of Los Angeles winked up at him.

He took a taxi to Pacific Palisades and his house looked good to him in the darkness. Once through the front door, he called out, "Anybody home?"

"Mrs. Ralston's upstairs," Annie said, coming from the pantry, wearing one of her sour looks. "Are you having dinner on time?"

"Hello, Annie. We can eat straightaway."

"I wanted to get home early tonight. I've had the back-ache again."

Nothing changes, he thought. "That's too bad," he said, trying to keep a look of exasperation from crossing his face. He reassured Annie and then took the stairs two at a time.

Carol was in front of her dressing-table mirror. "Oh, I wanted to be finished before you got here."

"Hi," he said, crossing to her. They kissed warmly.

"You must be exhausted."

"A little tired." He kissed her again, then got the suitcase and flung it up on the bed.

"I'll do that." She hesitated one moment to get the eyeline just right.

"There isn't much." He opened the suitcase and took out a large bottle of perfume. "For you."

She sucked in her breath with excitement. "Oh, darling." She kissed him again and then she had an afterthought. "You might as well confess."

"I should have married a dumber broad," he said.

"You wouldn't have liked that. Now, come clean."

"I went to an auction."

"There goes my bank balance. Is that why you stayed?"

"Well, darling, this was really something special."

"It always is."

"Honestly, this was a once-in-a-lifetime opportunity. Some baron died and they were selling off his entire estate. Books like that rarely come on the market, especially in one lump—and the auction was in the country, which meant the prices were right . . ."

"You are impossible. I don't suppose I ought to ask how much." His eyes avoided hers. "Maybe I'd better."

"Carol, these are investments."

"Why couldn't I have married an old-fashioned type that collected stocks and bonds?"

"You know how the market's been. Besides, everyone's buying *things* now, paintings, diamonds."

"All right, let's go into diamonds. At least they're not so dusty and they don't take up so much room. I mean, the house already smells like the basement of the Library of Congress."

"Now, don't exaggerate."

"How much?"

Ralston tossed his suits onto the bed. "These better go to the cleaners."

"The way you're acting, I really don't think I want to know."

"About twenty thousand dollars."

Carol Ralston's lovely blue eyes narrowed and then widened. "Who do you think you are, Howard Hughes?"

"He collects airplane companies." Ralston took her in his arms. "I *did* make some good buys. They're worth double here what I paid. And don't forget, after I fix them up, they'll be worth even more."

"All right." She smiled warmly at him and shook her head. "I just want you to know you're not conning me. I suppose I should consider myself lucky. After all, you might have collected spiders or something like that."

"No resale value."

"When have you ever *sold* a book?"

"Anyway, I'll tell you all about it at dinner. If we don't go down, Annie will have a fit."

"All right, Howard Hughes. Let's go eat. This should be a good story anyway."

They went downstairs with their arms around each other.

Ralston quietly slipped back into the old routines, both at home and at the office. He really didn't think much about the books until he received a telephone call at the end of the week. The customs broker said his packages had arrived, air freight, and arrangements had been made for their delivery the following Monday. Over the weekend, he found it difficult to repress his growing excitement, not only to see what the uncataloged cases contained, but also to begin restoring the other volumes.

Monday he telephoned home three times to find out if the packages had come. Finally, Carol told him, with an edge of irritation to her tone, "Yes, Baby, your toys have arrived."

"Oh, marvelous. Listen, I'll be home early."

"You didn't have to tell me. Are we dining in the cellar? Just so I can let Annie know." The light sarcasm did not disturb Cary. It was Carol's way of letting off a little steam. All women resent a man's being interested in almost anything besides themselves.

He was home before five. "Hi, Darling, have a nice day?"

"Just fine."

"Shall we have a drink?"

"Oh, go on down there," she said with a smile. "If I said 'yes', you'd have kittens."

"You're a doll."

"Don't I know it."

"I won't be long," he called back, as he headed for the cellar door in the pantry.

He dashed down the stairs with excitement. The two large crates, and a smaller box, were in front of his workbench. He took a crowbar and began to prize off the boards of the small crate. Tenderly, he lifted out the Zola, then the Dumas set, then the rest of his known acquisitions, and laid them carefully on the workbench. He was of two minds over whether to open the other cases. First things first had always been the rule of his orderly mind—but he was also a terribly curious man. He decided to take a middle course. He would open one of the mysterious cases, just look at the top books, and would then turn to restoring what was already on the workbench.

He pulled back the boards on the first case and drew out

a heavy, dusty book in battered condition. He blew the dust off, then rubbed the cover gently with his sleeve. His heart skipped a beat; it was Cobert's *History of the Reign of Louis the Pious*. With barely controlled excitement, he sought out his catalog on a shelf nearby and quickly flicked through the pages. Unless he was very wrong, the Cobert, restored, would bring in the neighborhood of fifteen hundred dollars. He already had a fifty percent profit on the first case. Now he could hardly resist the temptation to dig through the other volumes, but he forced himself to sit down at his workbench.

He selected the Zola to begin with because it required the least amount of work. There was some deterioration in the binding, which was to be expected, and the leather cover needed lubrication, but on the whole, the volume was in good condition. First he wiped the book clean and decided to give the leather a preliminary coating. He took a solution of neat's-foot oil, lanolin anhydrous, Japan wax, sodium stearate and distilled water and applied it carefully with a flat varnish brush, carefully avoiding the gold lettering so as not to dislodge the leaf. When he finished, he set the book aside and went up for dinner.

It was a week before he was ready to delve into the mystery crates again. This time he fished out two Dickens volumes, *A Tale of Two Cities* and *Nicholas Nickleby*, both in French editions, and probably worth no more than twenty-five dollars each. After his initial "binge," as Carol called it, he began to fall back on his normal hobby routine, working a few hours over the weekend and perhaps one night a week.

It was almost a month later when Roger Niles, their securities expert, stuck his nose into Ralston's office. "Got a minute?"

Ralston waved him in. "What's on your mind?"

"Cary, I'd like an extra clause in this merger agreement to cover the SEC rules on fraud."

Ralston wrinkled his nose and took the proffered contract. He studied it for a bit. "You worried about Rule 14a9?"

"Not worried. I'd just like it covered."

Ralston scratched his chin. "Well, this is going to delay things. I think I'd better telephone Du Pont. If we start writing back and forth, it could take a couple of weeks."

"Okay, and make it clear that we treat this as a proxy solicitation and not a tender offer."

"Right." Niles went out and Ralston put in the call. It came through half an hour later. After some reflection, Du Pont said he saw no problem, but would Cary send the proposed draft to him? "I am leaving for the South of France until after Christmas."

"Sure, I'll get it out immediately. It'll be in the post today."

"Excellent. By the way, I was most interested to hear about the Cobert you found. Have you had any other luck?"

"Small fish. But I've got plenty to look through."

"I don't see how you can be so patient. I would have emptied both cases five minutes after they arrived. Oh, yes, there is something that might interest you. Two nights ago we had dinner with Marianne's friend at the Sûreté. She finally squeezed the story of the baron's accident out of him. It was most extraordinary. When they found his body, there was no head."

"No head? Is that possible?"

"There is no explanation. I can understand why the Sûreté has kept it quiet."

23

"But there has to be *some* explanation."

"Also, the interior of the car was badly ripped up. Most puzzling."

"There is always a logical explanation."

"When you think of it, I will be most grateful and so will the Sûreté. They are baffled. It is very difficult for a headless man to drive an automobile, no?"

After he hung up, Ralston smiled. The French had a way of making an impossible mystery out of something that could be explained reasonably. He remembered Marianne du Pont's talk of strange things connected with the Baron de Chantille; no doubt this would add fuel to the fire. What surprised him just a little was the readiness with which a fine mind like Du Pont seized upon the impossible.

Sunday was a perfect day for a garden party and he and Carol were on their way to one at Larry Emerson's in Pasadena. He and Emerson had been close friends as undergraduates at UCLA and then attended Harvard Law School together, but in recent years, their lives had diverged; Emerson practiced patent law downtown and lived in Pasadena, Ralston practiced corporate law in Beverly Hills and lived in Pacific Palisades. They saw each other less and less.

Emerson lived in a huge, old Spanish-styled house, the backyard of which was rimmed by tall eucalyptus trees and had a couple of gnarled California oaks at its center. There were a number of people milling around, drinking and chatting in the bright sunlight. After about forty minutes, Emerson took Ralston aside, under one of the oaks.

"Christ, it's been a long time, Cary. You'd think we live in two cities. So tell me, how's it going?"

"Same old thing."

"Getting boring, isn't it?"

"Well, it does tend to be much of the same thing every day, when you specialize."

"I wonder how we got into this racket. I remember those nights in our first year of Law School, when we sat up trying to find out who owned the fish in *Ohio versus Shaw* and it seemed the most exciting intellectual pursuit in the world."

Ralston laughed, "But we know most of the answers now."

They went on discussing their respective practices until Carol found them; she had a tall, gray-haired man in tow.

"Darling, I'd like you to meet a neighbor. This is Professor Nelson; my husband."

They exchanged greetings. "Your wife tells me we live about five minutes from each other."

"Really. What brings you to Pasadena?"

"I asked him," Emerson said laconically.

"Oh, then you must teach law."

"Ancient languages," the professor said.

"Professor Nelson is actually an inventor," added Emerson.

"Of ancient languages?" asked Ralston wryly.

"Computers."

"Maybe we ought to start at the beginning." Ralston was a little confused.

"It's not complicated, Mr. Ralston. We made some innovations on computers that enter into our work at the university."

"That clears it all up." Ralston laughed.

"I'll try to explain," the professor said. "We use computers to give us the various shades of meaning a particular word or phrase might have. For example, the university might want to put out an up-to-date translation of, say, anything from *The Arabian Nights* to Plato's *Republic*. We run the old translations through the computer and compare them with other shades of meaning from other works. For example, our computer has in its memory banks the entire literature of Rome. No human could search his memory so perfectly or so fast." He stopped talking and shifted self-consciously. "I'm sorry. I do tend to go on."

"No, please continue," Ralston protested. "I'm really very interested."

"See, I knew you would be," Carol added, not without a touch of pride.

"It's the speed then," Ralston said.

"Basically, of course," Professor Nelson continued. "After all, it took Champollion twenty years to translate the inscriptions on the Rosetta Stone. He had Greek, demotic, and hieroglyphics to compare. With a computer, you could do that in weeks."

"Are you working on anything like that?" Ralston asked.

"As a matter of fact, we *are* working on Etruscan. Unfortunately, they didn't leave us a Rosetta Stone. But we've had some breakthroughs. I'm hoping that we may be able to shed some light on those mysterious people."

"How would you go about that?" asked Carol, "I mean, if you have no other language to compare?"

"All languages have patterns. We match the basic comparative structures of Latin, Greek, and so forth, to Etruscan and hope we can find some common links."

"You must be something of an archaeologist too," Ralston said.

"I *am* an archaeologist, Mr. Ralston."

Emerson smiled at the professor. "Did you know Cary here is a bug on old books? He collects them."

"Not old by your standards," Ralston told the professor. "But maybe that explains my interest in your field. Do you think your computers are going to give us any exciting revelations?"

Nelson shrugged. "In five or ten years we might know as much again as we do today. We might be able to completely rewrite ancient history."

Emerson put his foot up on the wooden bench that ran round the oak. "There're so many things. We're just discovering acupuncture. The Chinese have known about it for centuries. Do you ever think about how much the human race has forgotten?"

"That's another advantage with a computer," Nelson interjected. "They have better memories than we do."

"Fascinating. It's really fascinating," Ralston said. "I'd really like to talk to you about this at length sometime."

"Anytime, Mr. Ralston. Since you're so close to the university, why don't you drop by sometime and have a look?"

"I'd love to."

Ralston put his arm around Carol's shoulder. As they strolled back towards the barbecue, none of them realized that this chance meeting would lead Ralston into the most dangerous experience of his life.

During the following weeks, Ralston continued to work on his acquisitions. He finished the first case without finding anything more of value. The second case started with disappointment—it was a clutter of ordinary travel books, maps, and museum pamphlets describing exhibitions and various objects. It was not until a Saturday in mid-February that he came across the huge volume at the bottom.

It was a day of heavy storms which rolled in across the Pacific and had been drenching Southern California with torrential rains for the best part of a week. Carol had gone to her hairdresser and with his tennis game cancelled,

Ralston went down to the cellar early. He had just finished reworking an antique travel book of Italy. He removed a layer of pamphlets and saw the enormous book. It was almost three feet square and a foot thick. Ralston's heart pounded with excitement. There were no markings on the outside cover. Very carefully he set it on the workbench and opened it. His eyes rested on a language he did not recognize. The pages were very old. He would have to coat them to protect them from crumbling. With the most delicate care, he turned them one at a time, examining their condition. The first half of the book was written in the same language; written, not printed. And the last half was combinations of symbols, signs, interspersed with the same peculiar writing. At the very back, just inside the cover, he found a sheet of paper and notes. They were in French but he could not make them out. They seemed to make no sense where legible. In some places the ink had faded badly and what had been written could not be read.

Ralston puzzled over the huge tome for some time. Of one thing he was certain: it was very, very old. Before he started work on it, however, he coated the notes with a special solution he used to bring ink out, then put it under the infrared light. He could still only pick out a few words. "Mu. Necromicron. Book of Eibon. Unaussaprechlichen Kulten. Book of Pandemonium. *La pierre philosophale.*" Only the latter succumbed to translation from his English-French dictionary—The Philosopher's Stone. It rang a vague bell, but that's all.

He went upstairs to make himself a sandwich, which he took into the study while he pored through the encyclopedia and other reference books. The doorbell rang. Larry Emerson was standing in the alcove, soaking wet, shaking out his umbrella. Behind him the rain was gushing down, splattering up from puddles in the driveway, and racing down the street carrying mud and debris from the hills.

"Lovely day." Emerson left his umbrella standing against the wall.

"What brings you out?"

"Don't ask," he said, stepping into the house. "Some papers that had to be signed. The guy lives in Santa Monica."

"Come on, I'll give you a drink." Ralston led the way into the study and brought his friend a Scotch and water.

"Thanks." Emerson took a long drink. "Do you believe this storm? And they say there's another one behind it."

"So, what'll we do, build an Ark?"

"Don't laugh. I saw some nut walking down Wilshire with a sign: 'Beware, the Flood Has Come!'" Emerson settled into a red leather armchair. "I hope you don't mind my stopping by."

"Mind? I'm delighted."

"What have you been up to?"

"Nothing much. I've been down in the cellar fooling around with books. Hey, have you ever heard of The Philosopher's Stone?"

Emerson thought for a moment. "Something to do with alchemy, I think. That's right. It was what they got when they performed all their experiments right. It turned base metal into gold. Something like that. Why?"

Ralston told him about the book and the notes. Emerson asked to see them and they went down to the cellar.

Emerson nodded appreciatively. "Big, isn't it?"

Ralston opened the book. "Look at the writing."

Emerson peered. "What is it?"

"I haven't a clue."

Ralston switched on the infrared and looked down at the notes. Very little more had come out. He would have to try other solutions to bring out the writing. "Have you ever heard of Mu?"

"Moo?"

"M–u," Ralston spelled it.

"Nope."

"How about Necromicron? Book of Eibon? This one I can't pronounce. I think it's German. Unaussaprechlichen Kulten," he felt his way through the pronunciation. "Book of Pandemonium?"

"Nope."

"I can't find anything in the encyclopedia."

"Thanks for the compliment, Cary. If you can't find it in the *Britannica*, ask old Emerson."

Ralston laughed. They went back upstairs. They were talking about nothing in particular when Emerson suddenly said: "Say, what about Professor Nelson?"

"Who?"

"You remember. You met him at my garden party. He's an expert in ancient languages."

"Say, *that's* an idea."

Ralston wasted no time making the call. "Why, yes, Mr. Ralston. I remember you quite well."

"Look, I know this is a foul day. But Larry Emerson just dropped by. I've come across a rather peculiar book and we thought perhaps you might come over for a drink and we could talk about it."

"That's very kind of you."

"I'd bring it over to you, but in this weather, it might be ruined. I have no idea how valuable it is."

"I quite understand. As a matter of fact, I haven't anything pressing."

After Ralston hung up, Emerson asked if there might be something around to eat. "I'm starved," he said.

"I think we can rustle up something."

By the time they finished their snack, the doorbell rang, and when Ralston opened the door, Professor Nelson was standing there in a voluminous plastic raincoat and a floppy hat. "What a day!" He took off his outer garments and shook them, leaving them draped on Emerson's umbrella. The sky behind him was darker than ever, the rain slating across the lawn in sheets.

In the cellar, Nelson's eyes quickly took in the shelves of books and the racks of chemicals. "You have quite a laboratory down here."

"In a limited way."

"It looks quite complete to me. Is this it?" Nelson spied the large volume lying open on the workbench. "What have we here?"

"That's what I was hoping you could tell me."

Nelson frowned. "Can I turn a few pages?"

"Yes, but be very gentle. It's brittle."

With exquisite care, Nelson studied a few leaves; then he looked up and removed his glasses. "I don't know it."

"Can't you even make an educated guess?" asked Ralston.

Nelson put his glasses back on and peered at the writing again. "There's a certain similarity to Arabic, very early too. But it's not the same."

"The baron used to travel in the Middle East," Ralston said, remembering. "It *could* have come from there."

"How old would you say the book is?" Emerson asked.

"That's probably more Mr. Ralston's line, but I'd guess around the tenth century."

Ralston turned several pages until he reached the symbols. "What about those?"

Nelson studied them very closely and looked up even

more puzzled. They scanned the last pages together. "Here." He was pointing to one symbol. "Have you got a magnifying glass?"

Ralston handed him one.

"This one," he said, tapping his finger on the symbol, "could be Imhotep. Still, it's not the usual thing. But maybe close enough. Hard to say."

"What is Imhotep?" Emerson said, scratching his head.

"Who, you mean. Imhotep was an Egyptian of about 3000 B.C. He was a famous physician, architect, builder of pyramids, a genius. There was a cult that grew up around him, magic or science, hard to say what."

"I found some notes in the back." Ralston flicked on the infrared and Nelson leaned close.

"I can't tell you much. I'll do the best I can."

"Anything at all," Ralston said hopefully.

"These are mostly legends. Mu was another lost civilization. The story's very much like Atlantis, except it was in the Pacific. The Philosopher's Stone had to do with alchemy."

"Maybe we should go back to the study?" said Emerson. "It's more comfortable up there."

"You mean, the booze is there," Ralston said with a chuckle.

"I'm glad you mentioned that."

Upstairs, Ralston stoked the fire and it blazed up comfortably. "You know, when I was in France, they told me the baron who used to own that book dabbled in the black arts."

"Oh, rubbish," said Emerson.

"I quite agree. I'm just trying to lay out the facts so we know what I have down there."

"Rubbish?" Nelson said, slowly and deliberately beginning to fill his pipe. "I don't mean to suggest I believe in magic. But magic is sometimes another name for science. Alchemy, after all, was the mother of chemistry. Who knows what mankind has forgotten? You remember, I mentioned Imhotep downstairs. Well, during his time the Egyptians performed trepaning operations, brain surgery, a fairly advanced concept for 3000 B.C. That knowledge was lost and rediscovered only recently."

Nelson puffed on his pipe and then punctuated the air with it. "Remember too that yesterday's heresy is today's orthodoxy. Alchemists tried to turn base metal into gold. Today, that is theoretically possible, by altering the atomic number." He stabbed at the air with his pipe again, "So let me put this to you. Did the alchemist understand atomic structure?"

"I see your point," Ralston said, "but it seems a little farfetched."

"Possibly," Nelson concurred. "I only know this. 'History' is only three, maybe four, thousand years old. But of that, only the last few hundred years is really documented. There are huge gaps. And before that, man was on this planet for a million or more years. One hundred years ago, the horse was our main mode of transportation. Today we fly to the moon and back."

Emerson, who had been sitting back, taking it all in, suddenly leaned forward. "In other words, in that million or so years, there could have been a lost civilization?"

"Mind you," Nelson said, "I'm only speculating. Suppose there was an atomic war today. Everything would be destroyed—maybe not all life, but very likely all civilization. In a thousand years, what would be left? A few ruins? In thirty thousand years? Perhaps all traces of our civilization would be irrevocably lost. That destruction could also have occurred because of an ice age or because of some other natural disaster.

"But what if someone did escape, someone with knowledge, who passed it on from generation to generation. And generation after generation there would be slight distortions.

"Suppose an Einstein had lived a hundred thousand years ago? Imhotep was a genius in ancient Egypt. What did he discover?"

"I don't know," Ralston shook his head. "It seems to me that if there had been a lost civilization, there would have been some trace of it."

"Not necessarily. Natural disasters could have totally destroyed it."

The rain slashed against the windows and rattled the panes. Ralston got up to stoke the fire. "But does this have anything to do with my book?"

"It has to do with those notes," Emerson said.

"But we don't know for sure if the notes *do* have a connection with the book."

"It's a reasonable guess, Cary."

"Okay, and it's also reasonable to suppose the baron wrote them. If Professor Nelson here doesn't recognize the language, I don't see how the baron would have."

"I don't know anything," Nelson said dryly. "Let's put this in perspective. We have no idea if the notes relate to the book, or if they do, whether they are not merely speculation on the part of this baron. But I *am* curious about two things. First, I am always interested when a totally new form of language shows up. And second, I am fascinated by the use of the symbols."

"I only want to find out if it's worth something. I'm just greedy, that's all."

"I can understand your feelings, Mr. Ralston. I wish I could help. Perhaps, if you'd let me have the book, I might come up with something."

34

"I'd be most grateful to you, but first I have to restore it. Then you can certainly have it."

"The way you two go on," Emerson said, "you might have the Rosetta Stone down there."

"You never know," Nelson laughed.

CHAPTER THREE

◎

It was a lazy, warm afternoon. Ralston guided his Mercedes-Benz along Sunset Boulevard. The Santa Monica mountains, the houses nestled in them, and the spread of Los Angeles to the south were sharply outlined against a pale blue sky. On the seat beside him was the monstrous book carefully wrapped in a plastic cover. It had taken him a month to work through the many pages, alleviating the brittleness and then coating them with a preservative solution. He turned into the UCLA campus. The red-brick buildings baked in the hot sun. He parked in the shade of some trees and started toward the Humanities Building.

The building had an antiseptic impersonality that depressed him. He shifted his heavy burden and took the elevator to the third floor, which looked exactly like the first. Nelson's office was a tiny cubicle numbered 3345. It was a clutter of books, strewn across the desk, on the floor, in the midst of which sat the professor himself, deeply engrossed. Ralston knocked.

Nelson looked up like a man waking from sleep. He stared at Ralston blankly for a moment. "Oh, Mr. Ralston, forgive me."

"You *were* expecting me?"

"Yes, indeed." He picked his way across the floor between the books. "How are you? Here, let's make some room for that." He moved the piles on his desk about and Ralston set down the heavy volume in the space provided.

"That's a relief."

"I'd forgotten how big it was."

Nelson turned his attention to the book. "I know this might be valuable so we won't take any chances with it. We'll work from photocopies."

"Fine."

"You can pick the original up sometime next week."

Ralston had a better thought. "Look, if you'd like to bring it by Saturday, we could have lunch by the pool, have a swim, and maybe talk a bit?"

"That's very kind of you. I'd enjoy that very much."

"Good." Ralston glanced around the office. "You know, you promised to show me around here. If you've got a moment, I'd be most interested."

Nelson stepped past Ralston and the lawyer followed him back to the elevator. They went down to the basement, walked along the corridor and turned several corners. The lab was a large oblong room; one wall was a blackboard. There were several desks and small tables, on one of which was a slide projector. But the room was dominated by the computer, around which five men, in white cotton lab coats, were busy.

"That's not all of it," Nelson said, pointing to the computer. "The big one's in Santa Barbara. But we're connected up."

"Then you share time."

"Yes, with the whole university. It's a good system, really." However, the tone of his voice indicated it was a compromise at best, but nonetheless one that Nelson understood and accepted.

"Basically," Nelson said, "what we do first is to try and find a pattern. Every language has one. We also have to look for certain basic words: mother, father, man, woman, day, night. Words like that *must* appear." He went on into what Ralston suspected might be an oft-repeated lecture.

When the professor paused Ralston said, "It sounds very complicated."

Nelson seemed ready to resume his talk but one of the white-coated assistants interrupted.

Nelson turned. "Yes?"

"Telephone, sir. A Mr. Ferguesson."

Nelson's face darkened. "Excuse me," he said, as he went to the other end of the room and picked up the telephone. Even though Ralston could not hear what was being said, it was clear from the expression on Nelson's face that he was very angry, and from the way he turned his back and spoke in low tones, that he didn't want to be overheard. Finally, he slammed the telephone down. He stood for a moment, then stalked back to Ralston. He continued showing the lawyer around the laboratory, but Ralston knew the professor's mind was no longer on languages or the computer.

Quite suddenly, Nelson stopped his lecture. "Would you mind coming up to the office again?"

"No, not at all."

Ralston followed Nelson once again. They said nothing until they reached the office and Nelson shut the door.

"I need help, Mr. Ralston, and since you're a lawyer, I thought you could advise me. Please tell me if I'm out of line."

"Of course not. Whatever I can do."

"That phone call I had," he said, his anger welling up again. "It's a son-of-a-bitch named Ferguesson who's been driving me crazy. Damn, but I'd like to tear that bastard limb from limb. I'm sorry. That's not very academic, is it?"

"What's the problem?"

"Well, a couple of years ago Ferguesson called about a painting my father had left me. My father was an art dealer. Anyway, the painting was a Dürer. Well, I don't know much about art and Ferguesson offered me a considerable price for it. So I sold it. Now Ferguesson claims it's a fake. He wants his money back."

"Is it a fake?"

"I've had several expert opinions. They disagree, but the best experts seem to think it *is* a fake."

"Is there some reason you don't want to buy it back?"

"I don't have the money. When he bought the painting from me a couple of years ago, I used it to buy my house. But that's not the whole problem. Ferguesson is accusing me of fraud. He says I'm a criminal . . ." The professor's choler began to rise again.

"Would you like me to look into it?"

"If you would." Nelson spoke with obvious relief. "The truth of the matter is, I really don't have the money to fight a lawsuit. I mean, how much would it cost?"

"Let's not worry about the fee. Call it quid pro quo for helping me with that book of mine." Ralston pointed to it.

"That's really too much to ask."

"Let me worry about that, will you? And we're not involved in a lawsuit yet, anyway. If it starts to get expensive, I'll let you know well in advance. Okay?"

"I hardly know what to say."

"Forget it. Have you got Ferguesson's address?"

"No, I'm afraid I don't. But his name's Creighton Ferguesson. He's in the book, I'm sure. Beverly Hills."

"I'll get in touch with him. Usually, a nice friendly

telephone call from a lawyer is all that is necessary. In the meantime, you stop worrying about it."

"I'll try."

"Tell you what, I'll see if I can get through to him this afternoon."

Ralston left the professor more assured and drove home. Carol was sunning herself by the swimming pool.

"How about a swim?" she said.

"Soon as I make a call and change."

"Jim and Nancy are coming over for tennis."

Ralston walked up to the house and went into the study. He took the orange Beverly Hills phone book from the desk and looked up Creighton F. Ferguesson.

"This is Ferguesson." The voice was gruff, harsh, and ill-mannered.

"Mr. Ferguesson, my name's Cary Ralston. I'm an attorney representing Professor Nelson . . ."

"So that thieving bastard got himself a lawyer?" The accent was rough and Ralston surmised it probably sprang out of New York.

"Professor Nelson has retained me to look into the matter of the painting you bought from him. Now . . ."

"Look, what'ya bothering me for?"

"I'm trying to work out some solution, Mr. Ferguesson."

"Let that bastard pay me what he owes me and maybe I won't send him to jail."

"I don't think we're going to get very far by name-calling. And if you'll look at this objectively, Mr. Ferguesson, I'm sure you'll agree that there's very little likelihood of sending Professor Nelson to jail."

"I don't know about that. All I know is that painting is a counterfeit. I bought it in good faith. I've been trying to get my money back for two years and Nelson just cocked around with excuses. The painting's a fake and I don't like

40

being cheated. He can sell his fucking house and give me my money. I'll see that bastard in jail and in any case, I don't think the university would like a messy lawsuit very much. Tell *that* to Nelson."

"That sounds very much like extortion."

"I don't give a damn what you think it sounds like. That bastard cheated me. I want my money back and if I don't get it right away, there's going to be one hell of a stink, do I make myself clear?"

"Very. Perhaps if I spoke with your attorney we could come to some arrangement. You do have an attorney?"

"I don't need no lawyer. I can handle this myself."

"If you insist. But you'll have to handle it with me. In the meantime, Mr. Ferguesson, I suggest you do not get in touch with Professor Nelson regarding this matter."

"Don't you tell me what to do. I'll bother the hell out of him if I want."

"You'll only force me to go into court and get a restraining order."

"Don't threaten me," he said, his tone low and ominous.

"I'm not threatening you. I'm merely telling you what I will do if you continue to harass Professor Nelson." Ralston was finding it difficult to keep his own temper under control.

"I wonder what the bar association would think of your approach. What's your name again?"

"Ralston. Cary Ralston. I'm at 556 North Camden Drive."

"556."

"That's right."

"Maybe I'll have my lawyer call you and maybe I won't. But I'll tell you this, if you represent Nelson you're probably some kind of shyster and I know how to handle shysters." Ferguesson hung up abruptly.

41

Ralston sat staring in disbelief at the telephone before finally putting it down. Even a saint would feel like murdering Ferguesson.

Exactly a week later, Ralston was lounging by the pool, trying to concentrate on a contract, when Annie brought Nelson out. Ralston extended his hand.

"I left the book in your study."

"Marvelous. You finished photocopying it then?"

"Oh, yes. Wednesday."

"How about a swim before lunch?"

"Great." Nelson disappeared into the cabana to change and when he reappeared, he showed a surprisingly rugged physique. Ralston concluded that archaeologists who worked in the field under tough conditions had to be hardy specimens. The professor dived into the pool without any prompting and swam a couple of lengths.

"Have you heard anything from Ferguesson?" Nelson asked, when he came up for air finally.

"Not a thing, not from him and not from his lawyer. I think we might have put the fear of God in him."

"I hope so. What do you think he'll do?"

"I don't know. But as I told you on the phone, I advised him we'd get a restraining order if he kept bothering you. If he's talked to his lawyer, he probably was told to lay off."

"He could still sue me."

"He could. Anybody can file a lawsuit but it's something else to win it. We'll worry about that when the time comes."

"I don't think he'll just drop it."

"It depends on how strong his case is. His lawyers are probably assessing the situation. They'll get in touch before they sue. But I almost hope Ferguesson forces us to get a restraining order because, if he does sue, that won't look too good to judge and jury."

Ralston pulled himself out of the pool, dried himself off, and picked up the telephone. He buzzed Annie and asked her to bring out lunch. As usual, she made a few complaints but almost immediately came out with a tray.

They sat down to salads, sandwiches, and ice-cold beer.

"Well, tell me, how are you coming with our little project?"

Nelson leaned back and wiped his mouth with the napkin. "It's a damned bitch. At least, by comparing the form of the characters, we think we're fairly certain it's Middle Eastern." Nelson laughed. "That sounds pretty vague, doesn't it?"

"That's all?"

"Well, the book's divided into the written part and the symbols. We've got a couple of ideas about the symbols. There's a tie with certain mystical cults, we *think*. I hate to sound so vague but it's early days yet. We could be very wrong, too, because these symbols are not exactly what we've seen before. All I can say right now is there's a similarity. That could tie in with your baron's interests in black magic."

"Can't you draw any conclusions?"

"I can make some educated guesses. The language is not like anything we've ever encountered. It could mean a deliberate coding of something we do know or it might be an offshoot of Old Arabic. The best possibility of that might be a remote sect, some monastic group, like the Essenes. The Middle East's always had those."

"The Essenes. That's the Dead Sea Scroll cult?"

"Yes, but I don't think we can attribute this to them. They wrote in Aramaic, at least, so far as we know. But I'm not discounting any possibilities. You know, even the

Essenes dabbled a bit with necromancy, magic, and faith-healing. All connected."

"You still think it has something to do with magic?"

"Magic? Well, probably along those lines. A bit of magic and science maybe. And I'll tell you why. The symbols. As a matter of fact, on a hunch, I called in a couple of friends from the physics and math departments."

"What did they say?"

"They thought the symbols could possibly be formulae or equations."

"Is that what you think?"

"It's my number one hunch right now."

"What kind of formulas?"

"Math, chemistry, astronomy. It could be anything."

"What makes you think it isn't some kind of code?"

"It could be. But the language is already pretty obscure, very likely secret. Therefore, if you assume the language *is* a protective device, then why use symbols as well?"

"You're just assuming at this point."

"That's right. I have to assume to work up some kind of theory. Then I can prove or disprove it. If I disprove it, I'll assume something else. I'll tell you one thing, it's a damned curious book. I've never come across anything quite like it."

"I wonder if it's worth so much time. Doesn't the university worry about you spending their money?"

"They always worry about money. But I also have a deal to use the lab on my hunches. I've got a good feeling about this one."

"Why do you say that?"

"Two reasons. It's worth trying to find out anything we don't know *and* there is a tremendously varied vocabulary. You wonder how I know that. From the variations in character. It already shows a sophistication of vocabulary more complex than any early language we know of. It's on a level with Chinese." Nelson took the napkin and a pencil which was on the table. He drew "X." "Look at this." Ralston leaned over. Nelson added a stroke to the figure to make "$\underline{X}$." "The first X means one thing, the second one something else. That's how we can estimate the number of words in a language."

"I see."

"A complicated vocabulary means a sophisticated culture. And that's why I think it's worthwhile trying to decode the book."

The following Wednesday, Nelson telephoned Ralston at the office. "Can you come over this afternoon? I think I have something quite interesting to show you."

"Not until five," Ralston said, looking at his calendar. "What's it about?"

"Wait until you get here."

As soon as Ralston arrived at Nelson's office, the professor took him down to the lab.

"Look at this." He handed Ralston a plain white sheet of paper on which were written several equations: $K = \frac{1}{2}bc \sin a; K = \frac{1}{2}ac \sin B; K = ab \sin Y$.

"It looks like trigonometry."

"The area in terms of two sides and the included angle of an oblique triangle. That is what Professor Markham thinks some of your symbols mean."

"Then they *are* mathematical symbols."

"It's beginning to look that way. Now, it doesn't mean anything sensational yet. The Greeks knew about this in the first century B.C. *But* this is in the first few pages. Now look at this."

On the offered sheet, there were new equations: $\int_a^b f(x)\, dx$.

45

"That's calculus," Nelson said. "And now we get into some more sophisticated stuff."

"So what does it all mean?"

"According to Markham, these symbols progress from the simplest to higher mathematics on up. And he's only gone over a few pages! He said it's almost like an educational layout of various concepts such as we might do ourselves when sending a rocket to outer space, hoping to make contact with some higher civilization."

"What?" Ralston trembled with excitement.

"Now, don't jump to conclusions. That was probably a poor example. I only meant to say that this appears to start off as if someone were laying down basic principles before getting into really esoteric matters. As Markham put it, 'If I'm only into this ten pages, by the time I reach fifty it will be beyond my knowledge'!"

Ralston could not think of anything to say. His head was swimming. "It *is* trigonometry," he said glancing down at the page again.

"You know something about mathematics?"

"I was an engineering major before I changed my mind and went into law. That's why I do so much with computer firms." Ralston stared at the page again. He took up another paper. "I'll be damned."

"If you understand mathematics, perhaps you'd like copies of what we've done so far?"

"Very much. I really would be most interested. But I think I'm a little inadequate in this crowd. It's been a long time."

"Nonsense. You might just see something we're overlooking. The more minds the better." Nelson went over to the Xerox and fed in the stack of pages. He came back to Ralston while the machine automatically made copies.

"What really shakes me is this idea of Markham's," Ralston said.

"You mean that it appears this book is guiding us through the basics to some higher learning? He could be wrong. For all we know, later on it might degenerate into astrology. Anyway, I suggest you compare our mathematical symbols with what's on the page and follow it through from the beginning."

"How the devil did you crack this?"

"It wasn't me. It was Markham. Something to do with form, I'm not sure myself. Markham isn't very articulate in explaining these things. I'm beginning to have some sympathy with his students." Nelson smiled. "I'll send you copies as we go along. If you come across anything, don't hesitate to call."

"You can believe that!"

Ralston left feeling extreme excitement. For the first time in years he felt he was doing something really useful.

Over the next few days, he spent all his free time trying to sort out the puzzle. It was difficult going. He even scanned his old math texts to give himself a better grounding. It was tedious, demanding work, and were it not for his enthusiasm he would have tired of it quickly. He tried to explain it to Carol and then thought it easier to say he was working on the mathematical offshoots of a legal problem.

Meanwhile, equally involved, Nelson pored through the papers following Markham's lead. In a way, Nelson felt Markham was beating him at his own game. He had no choice but to sit like a pupil while Markham used the Ancient Language Department's shared time on the computer.

One night, after a particularly hard day's work, Nelson

returned home, his head crammed with equations, half of which he was unsure he understood. His head throbbed and he made himself a large whisky and then sat down at his desk with the symbols in front of him. He desperately hoped he would find something which he could bring into the sessions the next day in triumph. One thing was developing: if Markham was right, the writings between the equations were being narrowed as to meaning; they had to relate to the equations. If he could only crack the language, then they could race ahead. But despite all his efforts, the language still remained a mystery.

At a quarter to twelve, the jangle of the telephone brought him up sharply from the notes. He couldn't imagine who would be calling at such an hour.

"Is this you, Nelson?" It was Ferguesson's familiar, grating voice.

Nelson's heart sank. "Yes," he answered wearily.

"I want to talk to you."

"Look, Ferguesson, you talk to my lawyer." He started to put the phone down.

"Talk now or you go to jail tomorrow."

"Why do you keep pestering me over this thing?"

"Because you cheated me. And if you think you can get out of this with a fancy Beverly Hills lawyer, you'd better think again. Where are you going to get the money to fight me? You cry off being so poor. How do you come off hiring such a fancy lawyer."

"He's a friend."

"Oh, he's doing it for free?" The voice was heavy with sarcasm. "You're really an ass."

"Goddamn it, you listen to me . . ."

"Let me tell you something, chum. I got fancy lawyers too. Big ones. And they can make life miserable for you.

When they start sending you papers and dragging you into court, you'll wish you never started this."

"I didn't start this, you did."

"It takes money to win a lawsuit. I'll teach you a lesson for pulling this shit on me. I'm going to take it out of your hide. When I'm finished with you, you'll be lucky if you can get a job as a truck driver. When you get out of jail."

"I'm not going to jail. Ralston said you can't do that."

"Did he? Don't be too sure. Anyway, I got other ways of collecting debts."

Nelson exploded. "Don't you dare threaten me, damn you." He was trembling with anger and losing control, but he didn't care. "You better be careful, I can have the police on *you* for making threats."

"Listen, if you fuck around with me, you're going to get hurt. I got friends. The kind of friends who aren't too ethical. When they collect a debt, it stays collected. So you better forget about this fancy lawyer. There's nothing he can do to help you."

Nelson slammed down the receiver. The telephone rang again and he pulled the jack from the plug. He was fuming. Hatred seethed inside him like a thousand gnawing worms, boiling up and spilling over. He picked up the wastebasket and threw it against the wall. Then he poured himself a gigantic whisky and gulped it down. Then another and another.

He began to feel quite woozy. He sat down at his desk, his head falling forward on the notes, while visions of what he wanted to do to Ferguesson flashed through his reddened mind. As stupor overcame him, he could see Ferguesson pummeled and slammed, bits of him torn off, the blood splashing across the Chinese table and over the walls. Ferguesson was coming apart, ripped limb from limb, and

49

then Nelson experienced a feeling of satisfaction which dissolved into euphoria as he drifted into a heavy, drunken sleep.

Ralston bounded downstairs freshly showered and shaved. With lively steps, he headed for the breakfast room. Carol looked up blearily from the newspaper; she was never very bright in the mornings.

"Can I see the front page?" he said, ringing the bell for Annie. The latter stuck her head through the door. "Ham and eggs, Annie."

"No ham."

"Bacon and eggs then."

"I'll see if there's any bacon."

"Do that," he grumbled. He took the newspaper from Carol, and scanned the first page. "WEALTHY BUSINESSMAN SLAIN. POLICE REFUSE DETAILS." Although usually he would not have paid much attention something made him read on. "Late last night, Creighton F. Ferguesson . . ." Ralston felt his whole body jerk with shock. "Jesus!" he muttered.

"What's the matter?"

"Did you read about the murder?"

"I glanced through it. Why?"

"I was suing that guy."

"Really?" she said, her curiosity aroused. "What do you know about it?"

"Nothing. Wait, let me read this." He peered down at the article again. "Late last night, Creighton F. Ferguesson was found dead, horribly mutilated, in his luxurious Beverly Hills mansion. Although police have refused to give details, it is known that the first officers on the scene were visibly shaken by what they had found. One admitted privately that it was the most brutal murder he had ever seen in twenty years with the force. However, when detectives arrived, they immediately put a blackout on all news . . ." The rest was background on Ferguesson, about whom little was known, though it was suspected he had connections with gambling interests.

Very slowly, an idea flickered in the back of Ralston's mind, then it grew larger and larger until he could think of nothing else. "My God, Nelson wouldn't!"

CHAPTER FOUR

◎

Ralston pushed himself up from the breakfast table decisively. "Excuse me, Darling."

"Hey, you can't leave without telling me what's happening."

But he was already out of the room and on his way to the study telephone. A tired, stunned voice came on the line. "Ralston?"

"Professor, do you know what's happened?"

"God . . ." There was sobbing on the other end of the line.

"Listen, Nelson, would you like me to come over?"

"Y-yes."

"Are you all right?"

"I don't know. Can you come right away?" Nelson's voice had an edge of hysteria which warned Ralston there was no time to lose. If the police came, Nelson was in no shape to talk. But what he was thinking sent a chill down Ralston's spine. "I think I did it." There it was; no more need for speculation.

"Give me the address."

"2453 Rustic Canyon . . ."

"Off San Vicente?"

"Yes."

"Listen. Stay calm and try to get a grip on yourself. Talk to no one until I get there. I'll be right over." Ralston hung up, called goodbye to Carol on the way out the front door, and went to the garage. He whipped the Mercedes out and drove a little too recklessly down to Sunset, between the manicured lawns and bright spring flowers of the palatial houses. Just up from the Pacific Coast Highway, Rustic Canyon was a narrow, U-shaped cul-de-sac, with a threadlike road running up the center; it was lined with birch trees and bordered by small, moderately priced houses that seemed in need of redecoration. He turned the car across a bridge which ran over a small culvert and stream and glanced at the house numbers. Nelson's house was tucked up against the hill under a big, spreading, scraggy birch. It was painted railway-car red.

The Nelson who opened the door was a far cry from the healthy swimmer of a few days before; his eyes were deeply sunken and red-rimmed, the corners of his mouth were pulled down with fatigue, and his skin had a grayish pallor. "Thank God," he rasped. Ralston went quickly past him into the house.

"You look like hell."

"I feel it too."

"Now what happened?"

Nelson looked at him rather vaguely. "I'm not all that sure."

"Well, let's start at the beginning."

"I don't know if I can remember . . ." Nelson put his hand to his forehead. "Everything's so confused."

"I'm here to help," Ralston soothed. "Let's take it step by step."

"Okay. Do you mind if we go into the kitchen? I was just making some coffee."

53

Ralston followed him through the house to the kitchen. It was nicely furnished, in a rather old-fashioned way; the jumbled helter-skelter of a bachelor's home. And everywhere there were books: open on tables, lying on the sofa, and lining shelves. On the kitchen table, the morning paper was open to the Ferguesson article. Nelson got the coffee and sat down heavily. He lifted his cup with shaking hands.

"I was pretty drunk last night," he offered as an excuse.

"When was that?"

"Oh, not until late. I came home about ten. I was at the lab working on our project. I brought some of it home with me and I was studying it. About midnight, Ferguesson telephoned. It was the same old thing only this time he hinted he'd have the Mafia or something after me."

"Did he mention the Mafia in so many words?"

Nelson thought a moment. "I don't think so. I honestly don't remember it all that well. But he certainly made hints that he had friends who could settle with me. It was clear what he meant. Anyway, I'd had a couple of drinks before—I often do before going to bed. I got very, very angry. After he hung up, I started drinking more. Heavily. I think I passed out."

Ralston was quite puzzled. "I thought you said you might have killed him."

Nelson seemed rather shocked at the idea. "Did I?"

"Professor, you have to pull yourself together or I can't help you."

Nelson drank some more coffee. "I don't understand. I did pass out, except . . ." Remembering, he looked up confused.

"Except what?"

"You'll think I'm mad."

"Well, if you are, that's a defense. Go ahead and tell me."

"Just before I passed out, I *wanted* to kill him. I imagined what I'd do to him. At least, I think I imagined it. I saw him being torn apart, limb from limb, blood everywhere, on the Chinese table and the lamps, everywhere. He just seemed to fly apart, into little pieces. It was horrible."

"Wait. He seemed to fly apart? Do you remember doing anything?"

"No. I was watching. I was a spectator. I told you it sounded crazy."

"Then what happened?"

"I woke up."

"Where were you when you woke up."

"In the study. I slept sitting at the desk."

"Where were you when you went to sleep?"

"Why, the same place," he said, remembering. "I was right where I was when I went to sleep."

"Go on."

"Well, I came in here to make coffee. I got the papers and then I saw that he'd been murdered." He blinked several times. "He *was* murdered."

"Yes."

"I don't really understand."

"What did you do after you saw the papers?"

"You telephoned."

Ralston thought for a moment. "What were you wearing last night?"

Nelson looked down at the clothes he had on. "Why, these. I was wearing these. I didn't get undressed."

"You were wearing exactly what you have on now?"

Nelson looked again. "Yes. Why?"

"Because if you murdered Ferguesson, don't you think

55

there'd be bloodstains? Look, in your dream, or whatever it was, you saw a brutal death, blood everywhere. Had you been in that room, the way you describe it, there would probably be bloodstains. Even the papers say Ferguesson was terribly mutilated."

"Isn't that odd?"

"Odd?"

"My dream and what the papers say."

"Your dream was impossible. The paper really didn't say much more than that the murder was brutal."

"I wish I could believe that."

"Nelson, did you have shoes on last night?"

The professor looked down at his stocking feet. "Let me see, no. I took them off when I came in. The grass was wet. The gardener had been watering the lawn."

"What did you do with the shoes?"

"I put them on the back porch."

"Let's have a look."

Nelson led the way to the back porch. A pair of mud-caked shoes were standing on newspapers. Ralston picked them up and examined them.

"It must have been pretty wet."

"It's not a very good lawn. It doesn't get enough sun and the gardener always soaks it too much. It gets very muddy."

Ralston opened the back door and looked out. He could see a pair of muddy footprints leading from the garage, along the walk, and into the house; there was only one set of muddy tire tracks going into the garage. He leaned down and felt the lawn. It was still soaking wet. "I'm no detective, but I don't think you came out this way again. If you went anywhere, you didn't use your car."

"Didn't use the car? I must have been too drunk to drive."

Ralston came back into the house. "Have you ever walked in your sleep?"

"No."

"I doubt that you'd start now . . . and I certainly don't think you could walk all the way to Beverly Hills in your stocking feet. Where do you keep your other shoes?"

Nelson took him to the bedroom and showed him. All the shoes were clean and dry.

"They're all there?"

Nelson looked at the shoes again. "Yes."

"Frankly, I don't think you did go out."

"I don't think so," Nelson muttered. "But then . . ."

"Then what?"

"The dream, it was so vivid, so real."

"A man flying apart into little pieces? Nelson, I've got to ask you—do you take anything? LSD? Marijuana?"

"No."

"No drugs at all?"

"No. Just whisky."

"All right, don't get insulted. I have to find out."

"Sorry."

"Everything points to your getting drunk and passing out and not moving from there, dreams notwithstanding."

"It was so vivid."

"Dreams often are."

"I even remember that dragon lamp quite distinctly."

"By the way, have you ever been to Ferguesson's house?"

"Don't be ridiculous. I wouldn't have set foot there."

"All right, then, have you ever been in the house that was in the dream?"

"No, I didn't recognize it."

"No matter. It could have been a room you'd seen in a magazine or movie sometime, which you've forgotten."

They went over everything several more times until

Ralston was certain Nelson was telling the truth; and the truth was that he'd come home, become upset at the telephone call, drunk too much, and fallen asleep at the desk. And although Nelson could do nothing but concur with the logic of Ralston's analysis, the vividness of the dream prevented him from accepting it entirely.

"Don't you think it's rather more than a coincidence? I mean I *dream* the man is murdered and then he is. And it's also very convenient for me. I had a motive."

"I talked to Ferguesson on the telephone, remember? I'd bet anyone he knew had a motive, maybe many stronger than yours."

"I suppose so."

"Look, Professor, you've got a hangover, you've been working very hard, you were under pressure about this painting—all of these things worked together to help your mind play tricks on you. I advise you to forget about it. And don't drink so much tonight."

"I suppose you're right."

"I *know* I am. I can tell you one thing, you gave me a fright this morning."

"You believed I could do it."

"No, not really—but there's always a possibility. The most improbable people often commit murders."

"You sound pretty knowledgeable for a corporation lawyer."

"I ought to be. Before I moved up to Beverly Hills, I was an Assistant District Attorney for five years. Now do you believe me?"

In Nelson's eyes, that made Ralston an expert. "Yes. I'm sorry I bothered you. What I need is a psychiatrist."

"What you need is to stop burning the candle at both ends. I feel guilty about that. After all, it's that damned book of mine you are staying up with."

"I suppose I have been pushing it a little. I just couldn't drop everything and work on it during class hours."

"I'm in no hurry."

"Okay, I'll knock it off for a few days. There's nothing much I can do anyway until Markham comes up with something more than a theory. He still hasn't *proved* anything."

"I haven't made much sense of it either, but then I don't really know quite what I'm doing."

"Oh, you've been working at it too?"

"Just a little, when I have a moment. It's a bit over my head."

The two men parted, with Nelson feeling much better and ready to head for bed. Ralston heaved a sigh of relief. He telephoned Carol to tell her everything was all right.

About two weeks later, Ralston was in the library toying with the mathematical equations. As Markham said, the symbols seemed to progress from the easier to the more difficult—or, at least, Markham's suppositions did.

Carol, who was sitting in the big red armchair, closed the book with a slap. "Enough. I think I'll turn in."

"I'll be up in a little while."

"I think you've all taken leave of your senses, fooling around with those crazy symbols. I'm going to split my sides when you find out that book's *The Arabian Nights*."

"You might be right, too."

She pushed herself out of the chair. "Since we have a free night at home, I'm going to get a good night's sleep. Tomorrow we have to go to the Ahmanson. And there's an after-theater party at Collie Heindricks'."

"My God, they live in Palos Verdes!"

"It's only about a half hour from the theater by freeway and forty minutes from here."

"Forty? More like an hour. Honey, we'll get in so late."

"It's Friday tomorrow. But you'd better come up soon. I don't want you nodding off at the supper table." She breezed out.

"Just a few minutes." He turned back to the equations and then decided to give it up. After checking that the doors were locked, he climbed up the stairs and went to bed.

He was dreaming about equations and symbols when he woke up—or at least, he *thought* he woke up. He wasn't at all sure the following morning. He vaguely remembered his eyes coming open in the pitch darkness of the bedroom and hearing Carol's heavy breathing next to him. It wasn't anything he saw, but rather something he sensed; something that was in the doorway of the bedroom, standing in the hall. He thought there had been a smell; an awful, rancid stench that made him queasy; and he seemed to remember the sound of huge wings flapping from the hallway. And that was all. It had upset him terribly. He was bathed in perspiration. But he did not get out of bed and very shortly after the experience, he dropped off to sleep again. In the morning, he could not be certain that he had really awakened during the night and the more he thought about it, the more it seemed that he had dreamed it. In any case, dream or reality, he dismissed it from his mind.

When he got to the office, there was a call from Robert M. Fernandez, Captain, Los Angeles Police Department. Ralston returned the call straightaway.

"Well, amigo," Ralston said. "It's been a while."

"I'm sorry, Cary. You know how things go."

"What's on your mind?"

"You remember I told you my family had a ranch down near Escondido?"

"Yes."

"Well, some developer has made us an offer. I wondered if you could look it over."

"Anytime, amigo."

"Well, I'll tell you what. I'm going to be out your way this afternoon. Could you meet me for a drink around five?"

"Great."

"I'll bring the prospectus and I can fill you in a bit before you read it."

At five, Ralston left his car with the attendants at the Beverly Hills Hotel and went into the Polo Lounge. Fernandez was waiting for him. They greeted each other warmly. The police captain was at his usual well-tailored best, looking much younger than his forty years; there might have been a few flecks of new gray in the coal-black hair, but nothing else to show his age. He and Ralston had often worked together when the latter was in the D.A.'s office and a close friendship had grown up between them. Fernandez was the bright young hope of the L.A.P.D., and slated to be chief one day, if a Mexican-American could.

They ordered and sat back into the plush seats. "My father is getting too old to run the place and there's really no one to take over. Charlie might have . . ." His brother had been killed in Korea. "Anyway, I'm not really a business type. I thought you could give me some advice."

"How many acres does it involve?"

"Twenty thousand."

Ralston whistled. "You'll get a pretty price for that."

"He's offered four million bucks."

"You might be the wealthiest cop in history."

Fernandez grinned and shook his head. He handed Ralston a file containing papers. Ralston promised to look them over and give an opinion at the beginning of the next week. Fernandez seemed happy to have the burden off his shoulders.

"I guess you like that fancy practice out in Beverly Hills?" Fernandez was still disappointed that Ralston had not stayed in public service.

"I do. It's not as exciting, maybe. How are things going with you?"

"Good. Pretty good."

"Something wrong?"

Fernandez leaned a little closer. "I've got a real bitch."

"A case?"

"Murder."

"If anyone can crack it, you can. After all, you wrote the textbook." As a matter of fact, Fernandez had written four. He was one of the best-known criminologists in the country.

"Not this one. It defies explanation."

"I thought you were the guy who said applied logic can get to the bottom of anything, in time."

"Maybe I did, once." Fernandez sipped his drink. Ralston noticed for the first time the strains of worry around his eyes.

"Come on, Bob. We both know you don't solve them all."

"It's not that. The damned thing's so impossible. Okay, a guy gets shot. Usually we have a pretty good idea who did it. Sometimes we can't prove it. Even if we don't know who did it, we can make educated guesses. But I've never run across anything where I don't know how it was done."

"When you eliminate all possibilities, whatever remains, however improbable, must be the truth," said Ralston, quoting Sherlock Holmes.

"That's just it, the whole thing's impossible. I really

shouldn't be talking about it, but I've known you for a long time. In the old days, sometimes you put me on the right track. But if I tell you, you've got to keep this under your hat."

"You know that."

"Okay, did you read about the Ferguesson case?"

Ralston stiffened. "Yes," he said hesitantly. "I thought that was in Beverly Hills. What's an L.A. cop doing on it?"

"Holmby Hills. The papers always say Beverly Hills. It sells more copy."

"The papers said he was pretty badly mutilated."

"Mutilated?" Fernandez grunted sardonically. "He was ripped limb from limb."

Ralston's hand shook so violently, he spilled his drink. He felt as though a dark wave had passed over him.

"What's the matter?"

"Nothing."

"I didn't think you were so squeamish."

"What do you mean, Bob? You don't mean that literally?"

"Yes, I do. Torn limb from limb." Fernandez frowned deeply.

"Is that possible?"

"No. But you can look at the pictures, if you have a strong stomach."

"No."

"I tell you the man was literally pulled apart bit by bit. And I mean pulled apart. This was no scalpel job. There was no explosion. We've covered every possibility, every angle. There is nothing we know of which could have caused those injuries."

Ralston was trembling. He found it difficult to concentrate.

63

"The room was a mess, torn to pieces. Sofas broken in two. All the Chinese art smashed up."

"What?" The words knifed through Ralston, making his mind reel.

"Say, what's the matter with you?"

"Did you say 'Chinese' art?"

"Yeah. There was even a huge lamp, like a dragon, bent double. It was really something. I've seen a lot of ugly things in my time . . . Korea, on the Force, but nothing to compare with this. Ferguesson was ripped up into little pieces . . . little pieces," he repeated, incredulously. "Fingertips . . . teeth . . . bits of skin . . . blood splattered all over the room. You know me, Cary, I'm used to murder. But I promise you, I was sick." Even the recollection seemed to unnerve the police captain.

"I . . . I can't believe it."

"I don't blame you. It just isn't possible. No human being could have done it. In fact, outside of King Kong, I can't think of anything that could. It isn't that we lack suspects. Ferguesson was a real son-of-a-bitch. But Christ, we haven't even been able to make positive identification. We had quite a job collecting those little pieces, most of them anyway."

"Most?"

"The head was missing."

Ralston shook violently. His mind was whirling and twisting.

Fernandez leaned forward. "Hey, why is this affecting you like this? Cary," Fernandez said, his tone more severe, "do you know something?"

"I don't know." He knew he couldn't mention Nelson. But how could Nelson have known what the room looked like unless he had been there? Ralston was frightened, though he couldn't tell exactly why. There were too many

64

ideas pushing and clawing through his brain, confusing him. Nelson must have been at the scene of the crime; but if he was there, then was he the killer? It was too incredible. And how, in God's name, could he have done it? And the missing heads. What was the connection?

"It's so crazy," Ralston finally said.

"Give!"

"Six months ago I was in France. I went to an auction: the effects of a baron who had been killed in an automobile accident. I was told about the accident by friends. The police were keeping it quiet but this friend managed to find out. The baron was driving along, suddenly swerved into the barriers, and his car caught fire. When the police arrived, they couldn't find his head."

"What?" Fernandez breathed uneasily.

"They said the baron was driving alone. It was also impossible."

The two men sat staring at each other for a long time, both trying to draw some connection between the two events. "Are you sure that's all?" Fernandez said, a hint of suspicion growing in his eyes.

"Yes." Ralston wanted to help, but he could not reveal Nelson's story. There was a lawyer-client privilege which prevented his doing so and the privilege was the client's.

"When was this accident?"

"I'm not sure. Sometime before I got to France, that's all I can say for certain."

"Who told you this?"

"A lawyer I was working with. Marcel du Pont."

"And what about the policeman he heard it from? Do you know his name?"

"No."

"I'd better call this Du Pont."

"I don't know if he'd tell you anything. I'm not being

coy, Bob. He said the police were keeping this quiet. He just happens to have a good friend in the Sûreté. I don't know if he'd even give *me* the name."

"Would you try?"

"Yes."

Fernandez took a small notebook out of his pocket and scribbled a few words. "What was the name of this baron?"

"Baron de Chantille."

"Spell it."

Ralston did. "Do you think there's a connection?"

"I don't know. It's certainly worth looking into. Goddamn weird!" Fernandez wiped his forehead. "Don't mention anything about Ferguesson to your lawyer friend."

"I won't."

"If the papers got a hold of this, there'd be a panic. People would jump to wild conclusions."

"Bob, you're absolutely sure there is no logical explanation?"

"I've been over all of it with the lab boys. There is no explanation. We've tried everything. We can't even make a reasonable guess. And the coroner is completely baffled too."

"But it happened."

"Yes, it did. And you know, I can't even prove a crime has been committed. About all we can do is rule out suicide." The police captain shook his head. "This thing gets stranger by the moment. I'll know more when I get the straight story from France."

"I'll do my best."

The two men parted, both completely at a loss, but Ralston was badly shaken. Fernandez knew nothing of Nelson's "dream." What would he think if he did know?

He would have to conclude that Nelson had something to do with what happened. That was the only explanation. Nelson had described the room; he had described the injuries to Ferguesson. But Ralston was also sure that Nelson had "dreamed" it. Even if one could suppose Nelson capable of murder, how could he have done what Fernandez described?

Ralston was withdrawn and worried that evening, but Carol didn't press him, assuming it was some problem from the office. He spent a restless night and rose early the next morning to put in the call to Du Pont, using the pretext of one of the minor legal points that cropped up from time to time on the merger. Du Pont was surprised that Ralston would telephone over such a minor matter. They disposed of it quickly.

"Have you been to any more auctions?" Ralston said after a pause.

"Oh, there was one here about four weeks ago. I only got two good buys. And you?"

"No. I spent enough on the Baron de Chantille's library. By the way, have you heard anything further about the accident?"

"No. I think the police have closed the case."

"No wonder. It's a tough one to figure out. Of course, that friend of your wife's might have been putting you on a bit."

"No. He wouldn't do that."

"Depends how well you know him."

"Oh, Marianne's known him for years. He's not the type who jokes."

"That was Inspector Grenier? I think that's the name you mentioned."

Du Pont laughed, "No."

"I could have sworn you said it was Grenier."

"No, no, it was Inspector Fleurie—but I don't recall having mentioned his name."

"Oh, never mind. It's not important. For some reason 'Grenier' seemed to stick in my mind. Anyway," Ralston said, changing the subject, "have you thought any more about coming out to California? Carol and I would love to show you around."

"Ah, I only wish I could, but not in the near future. There are so many things which keep us here. Perhaps, someday."

"I'll look forward to that. Nice to have talked to you and give my warmest regards to Marianne."

"I will. *Au revoir.*"

Ralston heaved an enormous sigh of relief. He'd got the information, but he was sure Du Pont would be suspicious, and eventually remember he had not mentioned Inspector Fleurie's name before. But that would be as far as it would go.

Fernandez put down the phone after Ralston gave him the information. He had also spent a sleepless night, trying to figure what connection Ralston had with these strange events. Ralston's reaction the day before had been extreme. It had to be more than hearing the story in France. Ralston had appeared shaken by the details of the injuries to Ferguesson and not until later, when he heard about the missing head, did there seem to be any similarity with the French case. There was something Ralston was not telling him, perhaps something to do with a mysterious client. Fernandez was going to have to find out who that client might be. But even if he found out, what good would it do? Any good lawyer would advise a client to keep his mouth shut. However, that made Fernandez all the more suspicious. Was the client the man he was looking for? And even if he was, how could Fernandez prove what he did to Ferguesson?

When the call came through, it turned out that Inspector Fleurie spoke English quite well. Fernandez dismissed the interpreter with a wave of his hand. "Inspector, this is Captain Robert Fernandez of the Los Angeles Police Department."

"*Bon soir, Monsieur Capitaine.* How can I help you?"

"Sir, we are investigating a murder case here and we have reason to believe there may be a connection with a case that happened in France last year. I am speaking of the death of the Baron de Chantille." Fernandez spelled it because he could not be certain of his own pronunciation. "I wonder if you could telex the details to me here."

There was a long pause. "As I recall, *Monsieur Capitaine,* it was a simple automobile accident."

"Pardon me, Inspector, but we have information that when the body was discovered, the head was missing from the corpse."

There was another long pause. "I would have to check the files."

"Sir, I can understand why you people are keeping this quiet. We have a very serious murder case here and there might be a connection between the two. If we help each other, we might find the solution."

"How did you come by this information of yours, *Capitaine?*"

"I'm not at liberty to divulge that at the moment. But if you help us and if it is necessary, I would consider revealing my source."

"As I say, I would have to see the file. I will telephone you back."

Fernandez had no choice but to accept the conditions. He waited in his office, not daring to go out for fear of missing the call. Of one thing he was sure: the inspector was being very cautious. There might be something to the story after all.

It was over two hours later when the phone finally rang. Fernandez snatched up the receiver eagerly.

"You understand, *Monsieur Capitaine,* I had to make certain you are who you say you are. *Compris?*"

"Are you satisfied?"

"*Oui.* We have to be careful. If your case is anything like this one, I am sure you would not want unauthorized persons to have the facts."

"I quite understand. We feel the same. We are releasing nothing to the newspapers."

"Good. The facts are these: On August 14, 1971, Henri, Baron de Chantille was driving his automobile along the Grand Corniche from his villa near Nice to the villa of friends above Monte Carlo. The car was proceeding at forty kilometers, about thirty miles per hour—not very fast. Suddenly, it swerved and crashed into the guardrails. Two priests in the car behind stopped to render assistance, but the baron's car burst into flames. They tried to get the body. Impossible. But both priests saw there was no head! Later, when the ambulance arrived, it was confirmed: there was no head. The interior of the car was badly damaged. One window was knocked out from the inside, on the front passenger's side, and the two rear windows were smashed. The seats were ripped to pieces and there was other damage *caused from inside the car.* However, the priests swear the baron was alone."

"Could they have been mistaken?"

"It is possible, of course, but I do not think so. It is true they are both sixty, but one of them has almost perfect eye-sight. They are sober men."

Fernandez tried to think. It seemed as impossible as his own case. "Did you ever find the head?"

"No. We searched everywhere."

"Do you people have any idea what might have happened?"

"No," he said, with obvious disappointment.

Fernandez quickly explained the details of his own case. "So you see, there are similarities."

"*Fantastique*," Fleurie murmured. "I do not know what to say to you. Every investigation we have made has run . . . how you say . . . into a blind street."

"Would you send me a full report, all the details? And I'll send you all we have."

"*D'accord.*"

"Okay, now there's a lawyer here named Cary Ralston." He spelled the name. "He's the one who gave me the story. He got it from another lawyer, a Frenchman, Marcel du Pont."

Inspector Fleurie spluttered. "He is a good friend!"

"Well, Ralston is a good friend of mine, too. But we have to find out what their connection is."

"I can tell you that Monsieur du Pont knew nothing of the case."

"Maybe not. But if you could run some discreet inquiries on both of them, we might find out something."

"*D'accord,*" the inspector said flatly.

"On the face of it, I don't see any connection, but there's some thread running through this. Ralston and Du Pont are the only leads we have."

"Right," Fleurie said sadly. "But do you have any theories, *Capitaine?*"

"None."

"I hesitate to say this, but there were rumors about the baron. It is difficult for me to explain. I am a policeman like you. I deal with facts. But these rumors, it was said the baron had dealings in the supernatural."

Fernandez didn't know quite what to say. "I see."

"I only tell you so you have all the information. Naturally, I put no confidence in these rumors."

"Okay, now let's keep in touch. I'll send you anything I get and you do the same for me."

Fernandez put the phone down and sat at his desk for a long time before moving. If anything, he was more confused now than before. Both cases were absolutely impossible. Had he not investigated the Ferguesson case himself, he might have thought Inspector Fleurie was quite mad. He was beginning to doubt his own sanity.

CHAPTER FIVE

As much as he wanted to avoid it, Ralston had an obligation to advise Nelson. And when he finished telling Fernandez about Inspector Fleurie, he telephoned the professor and then went to see him.

Nelson was bright and chipper when he opened the door. "Would you like some coffee?"

"Okay."

He followed the professor to the kitchen again. "Well, what's up?" asked the professor.

"Professor Nelson, you've retained me as your lawyer. It's my duty to advise you."

"You're very serious."

"It's a very serious matter. Yesterday, I saw an old friend of mine, a police captain. He's in charge of the Ferguesson case."

Nelson frowned slightly, but did not show undue concern. "Yes?"

"Professor, Ferguesson died very much the way you described it, and in a room such as you described."

Nelson winced as if struck a heavy blow. "God . . ."

"I have to know if you've told me everything."

After a few moments, the professor had gathered his

thoughts enough to answer. "Everything. But . . . I . . . I don't understand. I've thought about it several times. I'm sure I came home and got drunk after I talked to Ferguesson. I'm *sure* I dreamed it." There was such pained sincerity in the professor's eyes that Ralston could not help believing him. Still, he had to probe. "Professor, very often people think they've covered their tracks. But the police have many scientific methods at their hands; even a hair could place you at the scene."

"May God strike me dead. I'm telling you the truth."

"You're quite certain you had never been to Ferguesson's house?"

"Never."

Ralston sighed heavily. "Then how could you describe the room?"

"I don't know. I don't know." A trace of hysteria came back to his voice.

"Now, take it easy. You've got to trust me completely. I am trying to help. I've got to ask some nasty questions."

"Yes . . ."

"Have you ever had any mental problems?"

"No."

"Have there been any members of your family who have?"

"No. Ralston, what do you mean he died like I dreamed it?"

"Just what I said."

"He came apart?"

"Yes."

"But how?"

"That's something nobody knows, yet. Look, it is possible that the police will interview you."

"Do they know?"

"I've told them nothing. But there's always a chance they

might come across something, like your argument with Ferguesson. Or they might have found something to connect you with the scene . . ."

"But how could they? Oh, I don't know. You think my dream is pretty wild, don't you?"

"I don't think you would murder, not even in a rage, unless it was an accident. But when you describe such incredible events and the scene of the crime in a dream, well, it's hard to accept. This damned case is unbelievable from so many angles. How could you describe what happened and how could those things have happened?"

"I don't know. It's like a nightmare come true."

"That's exactly what it is. Do you want to try to find the answer?"

"Ralston, I tell you, if I had anything to do with that, I'd want to take my punishment. I couldn't live with myself."

"The only possibility is that you might have gone there in some sort of trance. That is, you might not have known what you were doing."

"You mean, I could have been insane?"

"That's possible, isn't it?"

"I don't think so. I was drunk, but I don't think I was out of my mind."

"I think we ought to get expert advice, if it comes to that."

"You think I'm mad."

"I didn't say that. But the law recognizes cases of temporary insanity. Even if we get over that hurdle, there's the question of how it could have been done. The police say that it's impossible for a man to have died as Ferguesson did. Is there any possibility that you know of some scientific means, something perhaps that you've heard about at the university, even if it's secret research?"

75

"Nothing. I really know nothing outside my own field."

"I'm stumped. Look, I'm going to have a chat with someone I know—a psychiatrist—and put the facts to him. Maybe he can come up with something."

"There's only one thing I can suggest. It may sound incredible."

"Go ahead, there's nothing that can shock me now."

"ESP. I mean people have 'seen' things, things that have happened hundreds of miles away. I don't say I believe in it. In fact, until just now, I didn't put much stock in it, but there have been fairly well-documented cases and they are doing experiments in it at Duke University. Suppose my drinking released this . . . this ability in me?"

"I'd hate to have to explain that one in court."

"It's not so crazy, Ralston."

"Okay, even if that was possible, how the hell can you explain what happened to Ferguesson?"

"I can't," the professor said, growing more confident as the analytical powers of his mind began to come into play. "But that doesn't mean, because you, I, or the police cannot explain it, that there isn't a rational explanation. There is always a good, sound rational explanation for any phenomenon. But let's start at the beginning. It is possible that I somehow 'tuned in' on what was happening, but didn't quite see it all. Perhaps the brain reacts to horrors even while experiencing ESP. Perhaps I couldn't face what was happening, and I blocked part of it out."

"I just can't make any comment on that."

"The more I think about it, the more convinced I am that is what happened. I have never had an ESP experience in my life. Why now? Maybe overwork, drink, emotional involvement, the electrical impulses that tuned me into Ferguesson's house through the telephone, I can't say. But something happened that made me see what was happen-

76

ing there and it *has* to be ESP. I did not leave this house. I know that. I woke up exactly where I fell asleep. I didn't drive and I couldn't walk. There are no buses at that hour. Of course, you could check to see whether I took a taxi. But then, how could I murder a man in such a way without getting covered in blood? Would I get into a taxi afterward? It doesn't figure."

"No, it doesn't. ESP." The idea revolved in Ralston's mind. It would certainly explain some of the puzzle.

"And even if I find ESP difficult to understand, I cannot completely write it off."

"No, I guess not. I suppose there have been many cases." Ralston began to entertain the idea more.

"Now, as to what really happened, I *know* there is some perfectly reasonable explanation."

"I guess so."

"There's no need to guess. There *has* to be."

Ralston was hardly convinced, but it was something to grasp.

"What do I do if the police come?"

"You don't have to tell them anything."

"I have nothing to hide."

"It's up to you. You'll have a hell of a time convincing a hard-bitten police captain about ESP. He's going to jump to other conclusions. On the other hand, he'd have a devil of a time proving a case. Fernandez said himself, he can't even prove a crime has been committed. However, it wouldn't be pleasant for you being under suspicion."

"I feel I have to be honest."

"My advice to you is to say nothing—at least until we have more information."

"But shouldn't I tell the police what I know?"

"Not if it puts your head in a noose. Everyone is protected against self-incrimination."

77

"I always thought there was something shady about people who used that excuse."

"Well, the law provides it, Professor. You don't have to feel guilty about that. Even if you were guilty of murdering Ferguesson, you'd have that privilege."

"I'll do what you say."

"Good. If the police do contact you, get in touch with me right away."

"I will."

Ralston stopped by Marion Hunter's bookstore in Beverly Hills on the way to the office, and bought a book on ESP. He scanned it that morning. None of the cases cited could be considered legal proof of its existence, but there was enough to satisfy Ralston of the possibility, however remote.

There was a bright, clear sun shining down on the grassy green of the Pebble Beach golf course. It glistened off the water with blinding intensity. Ralston held up his hand, Indian fashion, to shield his eyes, then chipped up onto the green. Carol was waiting for him.

"Bravo."

"All right, Carol. I haven't played for a long time."

"That's why I thought you ought to get away for a couple of days."

They putted out, and started for the next tee.

"Did I tell you Dave and Nancy Steel were up here? They want us to join them tonight."

They arrived at the tee. He looked toward the hole.

"An easy three wood," she said.

"For Arnold Palmer, maybe." He teed up. The ball looped up high and the wind took it into the rough. "Damn."

Her shot went straight down the fairway and fell twenty yards short of the green. They started down the fairway. "They're at the Fireside Inn."

"Who is?"

"Dave and Nancy Steel. They've got some friends in the Carmel Valley who're giving a party."

"That's nice," he said, absently.

"I thought it might be fun. I know you're not keen on Dave."

"Not wildly."

"But you can lose him at a party."

"All right. All right."

"You're a dear." She kissed him, then strode away toward her ball while he headed for the trees.

After the game, they went back to the Monterey Inn and showered. Then, just as the sun was setting, they walked out to the shore and stood there silently listening to the surf as the sun went down behind a patina sea.

"It's really beautiful," he said when the sun had gone.

"I'm glad we came. You were looking pretty tired, Darling. Is there something wrong at the office?"

"No."

"Has it got something to do with that book you're working on?"

"No. It's nothing, really. I don't want to think about problems now."

"You're right. It was stupid of me to bring it up. Come on, Dave and Nancy are due in about five minutes."

They hurried back across the lawn to the inn.

The party was lively and, as Dave had promised, just about everyone on the Carmel scene was represented from retired admiral to hippie. Ralston didn't really feel very much like mingling, so he flitted from group to group and

79

finally found himself at the bar. He had successfully lost Dave earlier in the evening and was content to sit sipping a Scotch and soda while the drone of the party went on around him. He was busy with his own thoughts when his hostess, a pert and attractive live wire, clapped her hands for attention.

"Everyone! Madame Vskaki is ready!" She clapped her hands again, petulantly, scolding those who had not been prompt enough in quieting down.

People started filtering toward the living room, but Ralston sat in the semidarkness of the bar until Carol came toward him.

"Don't you want to see Madame Vskaki?"

"Who is she?"

"She's the 'in' fortune-teller around here."

"Oh," he groaned, "not that."

"Come on, everybody," the hostess was calling. "Now who's going to be first? Harry, be a darling . . ." Harry was led to the slaughter.

Ralston followed Carol to the edge of the crowd. Harry was seated at a card table before Madame Vskaki, a swarthy woman who suited the part perfectly. She was dressed all in black. In front of her was a crystal ball. Ralston almost snorted in derision.

"Shhh!" Carol protested.

He nodded agreement and watched Harry, sitting there with a silly, embarrassed grin.

"Give me your hands," Madame Vskaki said in a low, husky voice. "I am getting vibrations."

Harry gave her his hands and she kneaded them, all the time looking at him with her dark, hooded eyes.

The only vibrations Ralston was getting were coming from the bar. Quietly, he slipped away. Behind him, he could hear the "ohs" and "ahs" as the crowd responded to Madame Vskaki's revelations. Ralston shook his head and kept on drinking. He was terribly bored by the whole thing. He always hated parties which needed some "event" to round off the evening.

About forty minutes later, Carol slipped up on the bar stool next to him. "You missed it. It was pretty good."

"You have any idea what time we might be going home?"

"Honey, aren't you having a good time?"

"Oh, I'm sorry, Baby. Forgive me. I just wasn't in the mood for a party, especially with a lot of people I don't know. You have to keep telling everyone who you are and what you do."

"You're not getting drunk?"

"It's a perfectly legitimate thing to do and I'm not driving."

"Oh well, I'll have a gin and tonic," she said to the bartender, when he came by.

"Good Lord," Dave said, coming up. "Where have you been all night, Cary?"

"Right here."

"Don't you want to have your fortune told?"

"I'll pass."

"Oh, don't be a square." Dave started pulling Ralston into the living room.

Ralston gave Carol a long-suffering look, but went along. There was no one left and Madame Vskaki was about to pack up her gear.

"Here's one you missed," Dave said to her.

She looked up. "I was just leaving."

"Then let's skip it," Ralston said.

Madame Vskaki stared at him with theatrical intensity. "Are you afraid?"

"I'm just not a believer."

She took his hands and they both sat down at the table. She kept staring at him. He felt like a fool.

"You are a practical man. Yes, you have the gift of logic. You are perhaps a professional man?"

Ralston kept a stony face. He was not going to give anything away.

"Yes. A lawyer." She looked up to find confirmation in his face, but there was none. "You deal with corporations. I see an office. You work with people in the electronics industry."

That was so accurate, Ralston could not help a slight start of surprise. Madame Vskaki saw it and Ralston thought he caught the hint of a smile.

"I see books. Yes, many books. Wait, these are not law books. They are very old. I see a workshop . . ."

She stopped. Her face became a mask of terror. She dropped his hands and sat there staring at him. It sent a chill down his back. She was suddenly bathed in perspiration.

Involuntarily, Ralston asked, "What is it? What do you see?"

Her breath came quickly and the look of frozen horror on her face shook even Ralston. He could hear the people behind him suddenly become silent. The woman looked as though she were going to faint. "Evil . . . evil . . ." The words came through her frothing mouth. Her eyes rolled up as she pitched forward, twitching. Ralston watched her with disgust, not knowing what to do.

"Stand back, please." One of the guests, a doctor, pushed his way through the people standing around the table. "Give her some air." The guests began to move back. As Ralston glanced toward them, he noticed a few gave him odd looks. "One of you give me a hand." Another man

82

stepped forward and helped the doctor. They carried the woman into another room.

Ralston was still sitting there, stunned, as Carol came up to him. "Darling," she said tentatively.

He looked up at her.

"She probably had a fit," Carol said.

"I guess so."

"You're not worried about what she said?"

"No, of course not," he scoffed, getting up and putting his arms around her. People were still staring at him as if he'd done something. "It's just a lot of rubbish," he said a little too loudly.

"Maybe it's time to go," Carol said to Dave.

"Might as well. Don't want to get back too late. Let's find Nancy."

"Go on," Ralston said to Carol, gently urging her to help. "I'll get the coats."

Ralston went upstairs to the bedroom, collected Carol's and Nancy's things and started out into the hall just as the doctor came from another room.

"How is she?" Ralston asked.

"She'll be all right. She's had a nasty shock."

"Shock? Come on, it's just an act."

"Not her illness, I assure you. She was as cold as jellied eel when we carried her out. No, the woman has had a severe traumatic shock."

"But why?"

"Well, these people, clairvoyants and the like, are very emotional. Their imaginations run away with them. It can cause a mental state."

Ralston smiled, assured, and started out. At the door he turned. "Did she say anything?"

"She was rambling; delirious."

83

"But what did she say?" Ralston insisted quietly.

"Oh, some kind of blither about 'evil, unspeakable evil'. But what the hell, man. The woman was raving."

Ralston just turned and went out. He said very little on the way home. The Steels let them off at their hotel and soon afterward Ralston dropped into a fitful sleep. The next morning he awoke haggard and worn.

"Darling, is there anything wrong?"

"No, of course not."

"You aren't worried about anything?"

"No, just forget it, Carol."

"How can I forget it? You haven't been sleeping for weeks. That's why I wanted to get you up here for a rest. But even that doesn't seem to be doing much good."

"Just let me sort it out." There was slight irritation in his voice.

"Cary, you used to talk to me. But you've become so withdrawn. Is it us? Is there something I do?"

He put his arms around her. "No, don't ever think that. You're everything I want." They kissed tenderly.

"I wish I could help. Was it what that woman said last night?"

"No."

"You were very moody on the way home."

"I was just tired."

"Besides, no one really believes that junk. She told me I had a mathematical mind," Carol said with a laugh. "I can't even keep my bank account straight."

"Darling, would you be upset if we went back tomorrow?"

She was disappointed, but covered it. "If you want to."

"I thought maybe we could drive."

That cheered her. "I'd love that. But why do you want to go?"

84

"I don't know, I just feel itchy. I'm not very good at sitting around."

"We could play golf."

"I'm not very good at that either."

"Just because I beat you. You'll have to rent a car and cancel the plane reservations.

"I'll take care of that. Are you having lunch with Nancy?"

"We're going to do a little shopping. You want to come?"

"No. I'll see you when you get back."

After Carol left for town, he walked down along the shore. The bay stretched away in a vast crescent, dotted with seaweed-strewn rocks, while overhead sea gulls screeched and wheeled. The surf rolled up with a gentle hiss, then rattled the rocks as it receded. The sky was a slattern gray. In spite of the beauty, there was something lonely about the place. He very much wanted to be back in a city, surrounded by people.

He kept walking until he found himself near the town and stopped in at the airline office. Then he went to a rental agency to arrange for a car. He thought of trying to find Carol and Nancy, maybe having lunch with them after all, but he didn't much feel like talking. He wasn't sure when the idea first came to him, and he wasn't sure why he surrendered to it, but he looked up Madame Vskaki in the telephone book and walked the few blocks to her house. It was just up from the village, next to a motel. He rang the bell.

She opened the door and when she recognized him, she was none too happy. "I am busy."

"I just want to ask you a simple question."

"I cannot answer."

"You can tell me what that was all about last night."

She opened the door a crack more. "Do not look any further."

"Do not look?"

"No one can look into Satan's face."

"Oh, come on."

"That is all I can say."

"Why don't we look into the crystal ball again and see if we can find something a little more specific?" Ralston was sarcastic. "I was a fool for coming here. I don't know why I did. I must be losing my grip." He turned on his heel and strode off down the street, absolutely certain that it was all an act with Madame Vskaki, and feeling utterly foolish for having gone to see her.

The next day was perfect for a drive along Highway One. The car was delivered to the Monterey Inn and Carol and Ralston were packed and into it by nine o'clock sharp. The daylight was so intense that the trees and rocks seemed unreal. They drove through Carmel, quiet and empty so early in the morning, and then out along the farther end of the bay, as the road wound its way through cypress forests and then twisted up to skim along the sheer faces of cliffs, the sea crashing across jagged rocks far down below. The scenery was breathtaking but had a bizarre quality all its own. As they got up higher, they could see the vastness of the Pacific, stretching out to limitless horizons.

Carol was obviously enjoying herself. They stopped from time to time so she could snap a picture, and it was almost twelve before they reached Nepantha. There were two buildings on the apex of a promontory, the higher one a restaurant. Ralston parked the car near the lower building and they went inside. It was woodsy but modern, a combination of two concepts that somehow did not work, and the wares were arts and crafts *cum* hippie. Nearby, in Big

Sur, colonies of hippies existed in the hills, so it was not surprising to find on the book rack a smattering of occult, Eastern religions, underground literature and philosophy. He looked through them with little interest while Carol dug through pseudo-Indian goods. Nepantha, Ralston gathered, was supposed to be an avant-garde trading post for dropouts; but it came out a patchwork, where the tourists could watch the freaks in rustic surroundings and buy bric-a-brac. In spite of itself, Nepantha looked like a supermarket of the odd, and very much the American way of doing it.

"I think I'll go up and see if the restaurant is open."

Carol was still digging through the ponchos. "Okay. I'll come up in a minute."

Ralston climbed the steep, narrow staircase to the upper building. He crossed the patio and peered through the plate-glass windows. There was a huge open fireplace and empty tables, but no sign of activity. He looked at his watch: twelve-ten. It couldn't be too much longer. In the meantime, he decided to explore up the path that led away from the restaurant toward the overhang. There were thick bushes all the way until he emerged into a small clearing, just at the edge. The view was more than spectacular, it was awe-inspiring. He stood for a few moments looking out to sea, then finally started back down the path. Coming up it was a young man, his head shaved, wearing a long gown, who continuously clinked finger cymbals. There was a large chain with a brass medallion hanging from around his neck.

"Peace," he said, holding up his hands.

"Peace," Ralston said. He would have walked on by, but the path was narrow and the young guru was right in the middle of it.

"Would you help The Brethren of the Sanctuary?"

87

"What is it?"

"A haven of peace."

"I'm sure." Ralston did not want to upset the instant guru, in case he turned out to be less like a monk and more like Charles Manson. "How can I help?"

"A contribution of money is acceptable."

Oh, yes, Ralston thought, that is always acceptable. He fished into his pocket and came up with two quarters. He gave them to the youth, noticing for the first time the pungent aroma that seemed to emanate from him. The guru stared at the money, not very impressed.

"What is this sanctuary?" Ralston asked.

"A place where Mother Earth is worshiped."

Ralston went into his pockets again and came up with a dollar. One couldn't be too careful with this type. But as he handed it to the mystic, their hands met. The young man pulled his away quickly, but not without the dollar.

"They!" he said, wide-eyed. "They are coming!"

"They?"

"But you *know*." He stared in awe. He seemed to want to say something else, but suddenly backed up a few steps, then turned, and went down the path in the direction he had come from. Ralston stood there looking after the disappearing young figure. A cold, clammy sweat crept over his body. What had upset the boy? He could feel a hollow in the pit of his stomach and there was an eerie coldness in his bones. Why should that harmless, inane remark disturb him? Everything seemed to unnerve him of late. Try as he would to fight against it, the feeling of disquiet persisted. Why? It could not have been what the youth had said. It was the look in his eyes; yes, that was it. It was his look that reminded Ralston of Madame Vskaki, that same combination of horror and awe and of seeing something beyond comprehension. Damn! He must not allow himself to succumb to the neurotic figments of his own imagination. There was nothing to be concerned about. Nothing.

They ate enormous hamburgers at the restaurant and then drove to San Simeon. But if at first the tour of Hearst's Castle took his mind off things, it later began to depress him—Xanadu in California, ghoulish poking through a dead world. They drove on to spend the night at the Madonna Inn, so expensively grotesque that it seemed like something out of *Alice in Wonderland*. He arrived home the next day with relief.

Nelson looked up to find a tall, pleasant-looking man coming into his office. "Are you Professor Nelson?"

"Yes."

The man opened a wallet in his hands. Nelson saw the badge. "I'm Captain Fernandez, Los Angeles Police."

"You've come about Ferguesson."

Fernandez was only slightly surprised. "You've been expecting me?"

"My lawyer told me I might expect a visit from the police." Nelson waved him in.

Fernandez shut the door behind him. "Cary Ralston."

"Yes."

"Then you know you needn't answer any questions unless your lawyer is present."

"Am I to understand, then, that I am a suspect?"

"No more than others. Now, Professor, it seems you were having some trouble with Ferguesson."

"That's right."

"Do you want to tell me about it?"

"I assume you already know."

Fernandez drew in an exasperated breath. "Professor, I can only assume, if you refuse to answer questions, that you have something to hide."

"I have nothing to hide."

"Then why not tell me your side of it. I already know most of it."

Nelson turned it around in his mind. "What do you know?"

"I know about the painting. What's your story on it?"

"Ferguesson bought it from me. Later, he claimed it was a fake."

"Was it?"

"Some experts seem to think so."

"And what do you think?"

"I know nothing about art."

"So you didn't know it was a fake when you sold it to him."

"I still don't know, one way or the other."

"Where did you get the painting?"

"My father left it to me."

"Do you know where your father got the painting?"

"No. He was an art dealer. I can tell you one thing, though. My father would never have left me a worthless painting. There was little else in the estate."

"If he knew. All right, so your father left you a painting assuming it to be of some value, and you had no reason to suspect it wasn't. That seems reasonable."

"Thank you," the professor said.

"I guess Ferguesson was pretty nasty about it. He was a pretty vicious man."

"Oh, he was. He used to telephone all the time and make threats. That's why I thought it would be best for Ralston to handle it."

"What kind of threats?"

"He said he'd have me in jail for fraud. And then, that last time, he even said he would send people around to settle with me."

"You mean hoods?"

"That's the impression he gave."

"He could have. He was that type. When was that?"

"The night before he was killed."

"He telephoned you that night?"

"Yes."

"About what time?"

"Just before midnight."

"And he threatened to send hoods to settle with you?"

"Yes."

"How did you feel about that?"

"Well, I was scared, of course. But I was also pretty mad. He'd been bothering me for a long time."

"Did you go to see him?"

"No."

"What did you do?"

"Nothing."

"You mean after being threatened with hoods you did nothing? You didn't call the police?"

"No." Nelson felt uncomfortable. "I . . . I wasn't sure he really meant it."

"You must have known he was a rough character."

"Not in that way. Oh, I know he talked tough, and he was a cruel man, but how would I know he had anything to do with gangsters?"

"Who said he did have anything to do with gangsters?"

Nelson was brought up sharply. "Didn't you?"

"Not that I recall."

"Didn't you say he was the type to hire hoods?"

"That doesn't mean he was actually mixed up with them, does it?"

"Well, I only assumed . . ."

"You only had the one dealing with Ferguesson?"

"Yes."

"Do you gamble, professor?"

"Occasionally."

"On the horses?"

"I play poker with friends sometimes."

"You don't use bookies."

"I don't play the horses."

"Do you bet in other ways?"

"Mr. Fernandez, when I said I gambled, I only meant in normal ways. But I am not a gambler in the sense you are implying."

"Then you didn't have any gambling relations with Ferguesson."

"I told you, the only connection I had with him was over the painting."

"Did you like him?"

"Obviously not."

"Did you dislike him strongly?"

"Yes."

"Enough to kill him?"

"No."

"The thought never crossed your mind."

Nelson hesitated and looked away.

"It did cross your mind, then."

"Not really, no."

"In what way then?"

"No way."

"Professor, if you lie to me, I'm going to find out." Fernandez waited until his words had taken effect. "Did you leave the house after you talked to Ferguesson on the telephone?"

"Well, no."

"Aren't you sure?"

"Yes." Nelson tried to avoid Fernandez' gaze. "I was drunk."

"So you don't remember."

"I didn't leave the house. I'm sure of that."

"What makes you so certain?"

"Well, when Ralston came over, he proved that I couldn't have."

"When did Ralston come over?"

"In the morning. After he read about the murder in the papers."

"How did Ralston prove you had stayed home?"

"Because there were only one set of tracks leading from the garage to the house. And there was only one set of tire tracks going into the garage."

"Why would there be tracks?"

"Because the lawn was muddy."

"Had it rained?"

"No, the gardener came. The lawn was still wet in the morning."

"Couldn't you have gone out the other way?"

"I rarely use the front door. I always go to the garage."

"But you could have gone out the front way, couldn't you?"

Nelson was rattled. He hadn't considered that. "I suppose . . ."

"Is that all?"

"No. I'd left my wet shoes on the back porch. And my other shoes were clean."

"And that's the proof."

"I was still wearing the same clothes I had on when I fell asleep . . . when I passed out."

"Really. Is that significant?"

Nelson was taken aback by the question. "Ralston thought so."

"Where were you until you came home?"

"At the university."

"What time did you come home?"

"Ten o'clock. More or less."

"Were you alone at the university?"

"There were two assistants working with me."

"But you could have gone somewhere before you came home."

"I didn't."

"But that would explain the tracks, wouldn't it?"

"I suppose."

"Professor, why did Ralston come in the morning?"

"What?"

"Why did Ralston come in the morning?" Fernandez said again, more insistently.

"I was upset. I mean, well, reading about the killing upset me."

"Why should it?"

"It just did."

"And why did Ralston go through all these theories to prove you hadn't left the house?"

"I don't know."

"Isn't it because, Professor, he thought you might have committed the murder?"

Nelson jolted violently. "I . . . I . . ."

"Maybe we ought to talk about this downtown."

"Please, I have classes . . ."

"Professor, either you tell me the whole truth, or we are going downtown."

"Listen, Mr. Fernandez, I had nothing to do with Ferguesson's death. But if you arrest me . . . well, you can imagine what they'd think at the university."

"I'm waiting. Why did Ralston come?"

"I told you, I was upset. It's not every day that someone I know is killed."

"And it's not every day that a busy corporation lawyer

like Ralston goes out to hold hands with a client regarding a murder. Now you've tried that story once and I didn't buy it. So let's go." Fernandez got up and indicated the door.

"Wait. I'll tell you . . . but you won't believe this either."

"Try it on for size."

"I had a vision, a dream, that I saw Ferguesson murdered."

Fernandez's eyes narrowed. "A vision?"

"ESP."

"ESP," Fernandez repeated impatiently.

"All right, I know you scoff at the idea. I promise you I did too. But since that experience, I have done some research into it. People have had these experiences. We don't know why. But they do occur."

"Not during murder investigations."

"Nevertheless, I can tell you quite categorically, that is precisely what happened." Nelson spoke with an authority he had not exhibited until that moment. "I cannot explain it. But I can refer you to books on the subject and to research that's been done at Duke University."

Fernandez sat very quietly. In all his years on the Force, he had not heard that one before. But he believed Professor Nelson was convinced. "You saw him murdered."

"Yes."

"Did you see who did it?"

"No one."

"No one. Then how did he die?"

"He just came apart."

Fernandez straightened. "Where did you hear that?"

"I told you, I saw it."

"Did Ralston mention this to you?"

"Later. But first I told him about my dream. Then later

95

he told me a policeman had told him that the murder happened just the way I saw it, and in the very room I described."

Fernandez tried to think back to his first conversation with Ralston and how shaken the lawyer had been. Then, he remembered. "The Chinese art."

"I saw it in the room."

"Describe the room."

"It was all Chinese. Chinese paintings and Chinese furniture. A long coffee table. There was a huge lamp shaped like a dragon."

"Was there a plate-glass window?"

"Oh, yes, overlooking the garden. And there were bonsai trees on the terrace."

Fernandez leaned back. "You saw Ferguesson just come apart?"

"He suddenly flew into little pieces."

"He exploded?"

"No. It didn't happen that fast. He just started coming apart."

"Had you ever been to Ferguesson's house before that night?"

"I have never been to Ferguesson's house, including that night."

"Either you are very naive, Professor, or very clever. I can't make up my mind. No doubt Ralston told you we can't make any arrests until we prove a *crime* has been committed. And to do that, we have to show *how* it was done. But I can take you in for questioning, so let's go."

"Please, you promised, if I told you . . ."

"I didn't promise anything. Listen, Professor, you have just about admitted killing Ferguesson."

"I have not! I told you the truth."

"If you really believe that, then Ralston can probably

96

get you off on a plea of insanity. Maybe that's what this is all about. On second thought, Professor, I'm *not* going to take you in, not at the moment anyway. But I'm warning you not to leave town."

"You *have* to believe me. I had an ESP experience."

"Please," Fernandez replied sardonically, "I'm a cop. I deal in facts. Just one more question. Have you ever been to Europe?"

"Yes."

"When was the last time?"

"About three years ago."

"You weren't in Europe last August?"

"No."

"That's easy enough to check."

"Then check. I was not in Europe last August."

"In the meantime, I'm going to have a little talk with Cary Ralston. There's something very funny going on around here and I mean to find out what it is. And believe me, I will."

"You suspect me."

"You're damned right, I do." Fernandez went out with a sour expression on his face.

CHAPTER SIX

◎

Unable to shake the memory of his two experiences on the Carmel trip, Ralston was worried about himself. It was not like him. He had always been able to set aside the most gnawing problems, but now he seemed to have lost that ability. Day and night images of the youthful guru and saturnine Madame Vskaki forced their way through to his consciousness. No matter how he concentrated on legal matters, some thought of Nelson, Ferguesson, or the Baron de Chantille seemed to intrude. He resolved to seek advice, but resolutions made in weak moments are not easily acted upon. Every morning he stared at the penciled "AG" on his desk calendar, then procrastinated another day. But finally, the obsession took over and something had to be done.

Dr. Aaron Greenberg was not only a client but a friend. They had known each other for a few years, but almost entirely in a business capacity. The doctor preferred investing his money in new business ventures, where there was some excitement, to salting it away in stocks and bonds. It was his one flamboyant trait; time and again he came into Ralston's office to have the details of some new partnership, corporation, or joint venture drawn up. Surprisingly, he had been successful on the whole. But business was not Aaron Greenberg's primary concern; he was one of the most successful and brilliant psychiatrists in Beverly Hills. His Canon Drive offices were soothingly furnished and boasted a couple of respectable modern oils on the walls. Ralston skimmed through six months of *The New Yorker* without paying much interest. He wasn't certain he should have come, but then the door to the waiting room opened, and Greenberg's pleasant, intelligent face peered through.

"Come on in, Cary." It was a different Greenberg that Ralston followed into the inner office. He was more reserved; not unfriendly, but serious. They sat down at the desk. Ralston glanced at the couch. It made him think of all those jokes. "I was a little surprised when you wanted to see me here," Greenberg confided.

"I know. Aaron, we've got a lot to cram into an hour. I'll try to make this as concise as I can, and not to color the facts. I'm here to get your medical advice, as an expert."

Greenberg filled his pipe. "Shoot." He was slightly bald and his high forehead enhanced his intelligent look. He listened attentively, but impassively, as Ralston ran through the events that had begun in Paris and occurred in Carmel. Throughout, Greenberg hardly changed his expression.

"That's it."

"Quite a story."

"I swear to you, those are the facts, as I know them."

"What do you think about all this?" The psychiatrist tamped his pipe and relit it.

"I don't know. I'm almost afraid to face what I think."

"I think you are. But anyway, Cary, what do you want from me?"

"I'm not exactly sure of that either. I want some advice. I need some help on the legal aspects. And I need some personal help." Ralston summoned up his resolve. "First, is it possible for Nelson to have seen all this by ESP?"

Greenberg ducked his head and appeared to be staring between his feet. Finally, he looked up; "Look—ah . . . this really isn't my field . . . but . . ." He paused for a moment and looked up at the ceiling, as if almost expecting to find the answer there. Then he looked back to Ralston. "There have been some experiments but the findings are not conclusive."

"Let me put it this way; do you think it's impossible?"

"No, but that's only a personal opinion. As a scientist I would have to say there's no proof. There's something else you have to consider, Cary. Was Nelson hallucinating?"

"You mean, is he crazy?"

"That's not a medical term, but . . . yes. In any case, I couldn't draw any conclusions unless I talked to him personally. The story he tells would certainly sound like mental disturbance, but not if you put any credence in Captain Fernandez' story."

"Captain Fernandez is no fool, Aaron."

"I've read his books. I was quite impressed. I grant you, as a medical man, I cannot explain those injuries to Ferguesson. But that doesn't mean there isn't some logical answer. Even if a man as brilliant as Fernandez hasn't found it yet."

"That's what we all keep saying—there has to be some logical answer."

"And you're beginning to doubt it."

"What about the French case?"

"Look, I don't have an answer. Cary, I think what you're trying to tell me is that there's something supernatural in all this."

"Don't be ridiculous."

100

"I promise you, the way you present this, there is no other conclusion."

"I haven't changed any of the facts."

"It isn't the facts so much as the way you interpret them. The real question is, how is all this affecting you?"

"It worries me. That's one of the reasons I came here."

"Can we look at that for a minute?" Ralston gestured his permission for the psychiatrist to go on. "Take the incidents on your Carmel trip. As a practical man, do you believe in fortune-tellers?"

"No."

"Wasn't it the famous magician Houdini who looked for honest mediums and clairvoyants, all the time wanting to find one, and who never did?"

"I think so."

"He was an expert and could see through their illusions, right?"

"Yes, I see your point. I don't believe in fortune-tellers; why did this one upset me?"

"Good. Now let's take that incident on the path. Here you are confronted by a young American very likely on drugs and you accept what he says without question. No, not even that . . . it's not really *what* he said, but the way he looked at you. Could you be reading more into these events than is there?"

"It's possible . . . but . . ."

"No buts. It's likely. Your mind has been conditioned by recent events . . . your equilibrium is upset and you are susceptible to suggestion. Look, didn't you tell me that the fortune-teller went into a fit and was frothing at the mouth?"

"Yes."

"Isn't that some indication she was mentally disturbed?"

"It could be, but all these things happening, all at once . . ."

"Hah, let me give you an example. If you were an escaped criminal, hounded on all sides, don't you think you might read too much into ordinary, commonplace happenings? It happens all the time. The hotel porter seems to stare at you, the post office clerk seems to recognize you, the bank clerk leaves the window—to telephone the police? The worried man interprets these things in terms of his own problems."

"Aaron, you explain it very neatly. But there are still things you cannot explain."

"I admit that. I also cannot explain a quasar or a pulsar, but that doesn't mean they are supernatural."

"That's different."

"Not so much. Men have always become superstitious when faced with certain imponderables. But let's get back to you. Besides these things which you have told me about, have you had any other disturbing problems?"

"No."

"Your marriage is fine?"

"Wonderful."

"There aren't any big worries at the office?"

"Nothing more than usual. I wouldn't even call them worries. There are problems." Ralston waved them off as meaningless.

"Have you had trouble sleeping?"

"Yes."

"Bad dreams?"

"Not particularly."

"Any dreams at all?"

"Well . . . There was one. If it *was* a dream. I mean, it didn't seem like a dream, but I guess it was. I woke up or dreamed I did. I thought there was something standing in the bedroom doorway."

"What?"

"Don't really know. I couldn't see anything. It was pitch black."

"That was all?"

"No, there was a smell. It's hard to describe . . . something awful, like terrible decay . . ."

"Did you hear anything?"

Ralston considered it for a moment. "As a matter of fact, now that you mention it, I thought I heard flapping."

"Flapping?"

"Like giant wings. That's about it."

"Do you have any idea what might have been in the doorway?"

"I told you, I couldn't see."

"But do you have any *impression* of what it could have been?"

Ralston did not say anything for a long time. "It would sound crazy."

"Let me be the judge of that."

"A bird, a giant bird, eight feet tall." Ralston flushed with embarrassment and turned his head away. "I guess that does it."

"What do you mean?"

"I suppose you'll call the paddy wagon."

"Cary, please. Let's say you did wake up. It was very dark. Any mind reacts to the dark with fear and imagination, because you are without one of your senses. Sight. Also, at the moment of first waking, the senses are still dulled by sleep. So, a curtain flapping could have provided the sound; an aroma from outside and your imagination did the rest."

"I don't know that the curtains were flapping."

"It's a plausible explanation."

"Yes," Ralston objected, "but Aaron, when you take these things bit by bit, it sounds different."

"All right, let's put it all in context. You have this mysterious book and this is the reason you got to know Professor Nelson. In discussions with him, he tells you about lost civilizations, necromancy, and ancient lore. You are not stupid and you are quite intellectually curious and imaginative. Well, there is the fertile ground in which you planted these other seeds."

"Do you think it's all my imagination, what Nelson said, what Fernandez said, and the death of the baron?"

"No. I've told you, I can't offer explanations. But I don't jump to conclusions either."

"And you think I do?"

"I think that you have carefully excluded all natural explanations, but cannot face the only possible conclusion you leave yourself . . . the supernatural.

"Okay, let me put it on the line. What do you think about such things?"

Greenberg smiled and shook his head. "How can I answer that? I'm no more qualified to speak about the supernatural than I am to advise you how to build an atomic power plant. I can give you opinions, but what are they worth? My guesses are no better than yours. I'm a psychiatrist. I deal with mental disease. All I can say to you is that whenever I have run up against the supernatural before, it turned out to be explainable in medical terms."

"Are you trying to say I'm cracking up?"

"Not in the least. But it is obvious that you have been derailed a bit—and susceptible to suggestion. You aren't the type to 'crack up' as you put it. But we all go through periods of strain and overwork and, during such periods, problems that we can normally handle become difficult to cope with. Our defenses are low—it's like being susceptible to a cold because we've been out in the rain. We all have these things buried deep inside us. The only way to really root them out is by analysis, but that is a long and costly process. I do not recommend it lightly. Let me give you an example. A few days ago a young man came in here. He has an unfounded fear of flying. But his job does not require him to fly. Therefore he can be afraid of airplanes and still cope with his life. However, if he were involved in international travel, then his fear would block his ability to function and analysis would be needed. So if dabbling in the supernatural bothers you, don't! Worry about the law."

"What if all this isn't a figment of my imagination?"

Greenberg spread his hands wide. "Let's take another example. You told me the story of Nelson's dream. Now let us suppose your friend Nelson has guilt feelings. He talked to the victim on the phone and wished him dead. Bang! the next morning he was. Deep down in his subconscious, he may think he's guilty. Perhaps this had happened before, in his childhood, and this new experience triggered a long-repressed subconscious drive."

"Okay, but how do you explain that he knew the way Ferguesson died and what the room looked like?"

"Do you discount the possibility that he could have gone there in a traumatic state which he could not remember the next morning . . . or that something happened while he was there, which his mind could not accept and blotted out? The next morning he remembers only what he wants to, and passes it off as a dream. I could give you any number of plausible theories."

"Aaron, I wonder, if you were practicing in 1492 and

Columbus came in and told you the world was round. what would you do?"

"I'd buy land in New York."

They both laughed.

"Cary, my best advice is to take some time off. You can afford it. Go away for a month and forget about all this stuff."

"And what if I still have it on my mind when I come back?"

"Let's see how you feel when you get back."

"Aaron, just one thing, is it impossible? Are there things we don't understand? Could there be a supernatural?"

"I think you have to answer that for yourself. Now, I'm afraid our time is up," he said in the stereotyped professional tone he used at the end of each hour. He stood up and walked Ralston to the door.

"You have to admit there are some puzzling things you can't explain about this."

"All right, I do," the psychiatrist said, "but it isn't going to cause me any sleepless nights. If you want to fool around with the supernatural, go to church. It won't give you bad dreams," he said with a twinkle in his eyes, as he shut the door.

When he got back to the office, Fernandez was waiting. Ralston could tell at a glance that the policeman was not happy with him. Fernandez followed him silently into his private office.

After Ralston closed the door, Fernandez said, "I've got a bone to pick with you."

"It was written all over your face."

"You're coming very close to obstructing justice."

"How's that?"

"Professor Nelson." Fernandez' gaze was steady as Ralston stopped, stared for a moment, then continued to his desk chair and sat down.

"He's my client. What of it?"

"He told me that cock-and-bull story about ESP."

Ralston's face drained. He knew he couldn't trust a gabby professor to keep his mouth shut and he didn't have to be told what Fernandez' reaction was. "That's his story."

"Is it his? Or did he have some help?"

Ralston didn't answer. The implication was unfair. The two men regarded each other with a degree of hostility.

"Not only that, I told you about Ferguesson in confidence and you blabbed it to Nelson. I thought we were friends."

"Nelson told me his story first. I wanted to see if I could shake it."

"Did you?"

"Not a bit."

"You don't expect me to buy that."

"What? My saying I couldn't crack his story . . . or his story?"

Fernandez didn't answer quite quickly enough to belie the obviousness of his suspicion on both counts. "His story. ESP! For Christ's sake, are you going into court with something like that? They'll laugh you out of town."

"Maybe. We haven't got to court yet."

"You know, Cary, I've got a terrible feeling you're setting me up for something. You'd love to have me arrest Nelson, take him down and pump him. He won't change his story. And when you question us at the trial, we'll have to admit that. So you'll have *police* evidence to prove your plea of insanity. And don't tell me you're not thinking of that. You were at Greenberg's office not half an hour ago."

"So you're following me. Maybe you think Nelson and I are in this together?"

"Do you believe that ESP story, Cary?"

"I'm not sure."

"You have doubts?" Fernandez asked, wide-eyed. "What do you take me for?"

"Bob, I promise you it's not what you think. You know everything I do now. Did you talk to that French inspector?"

Fernandez turned away. "Yes."

"What did he say?"

"Substantially what you did."

"So it's true," Ralston muttered.

"Don't try to blind my eyes with that." Fernandez stepped back to the desk and stared down at the lawyer. "I'll get to the bottom of this if I have to pull you, Nelson and Du Pont in. Nelson as much as confessed to me. He knew the details of the crime; he knew the scene. That's about all we need."

"You haven't proved there *was* a crime yet."

"No?"

Ralston got up and came around the desk. "Bob, you have to believe me, you know as much about this thing as I do."

"I was a little disappointed that you, of all people, would try to pull the insanity bit with me."

"Listen to me. Nelson was and is my client. I can't tell you anything he says to me in confidence. I'm on the other side of the fence now, Bob. But that shouldn't affect our friendship. I'm not pulling any tricks on you. I certainly don't understand what's happening myself. If Nelson told me he was on the moon at the time Ferguesson died, then I'd have an obligation to tell that to the court."

Fernandez seemed somewhat mollified. "Have you

thought about this? Nelson's a professor, a scientist. Suppose he knows about some new thing, something which he could have used to kill Ferguesson."

"In the first place, he's an archaeologist."

"And he also invents computers. You know he's patented an idea?"

"Yes."

"Okay. Even archaeologists know about a few things more advanced than a spade. They deal in many things, from radiation timing to sophisticated new equipment in underwater research. So let's not count him out there. Also, he happens to be at a university. He might have friends in other departments. He might have found out about something. You know, they do do a bit of secret research out there."

"Everything you say is true. But I asked him. He said he knew of nothing."

"He also told you he saw the whole thing through extrasensory perception."

"In other words, you think he's lying?"

"What would you say if we arrested a man and he claimed to have been picked up by a flying saucer at the time of the murder?"

"That's different."

"To you, maybe. To me, hokus-pokus is hokus-pokus. Maybe you believe this guy, maybe you don't. If you don't, then I guess you're doing your job. If you do, I don't know what to think. All I know is that Nelson may have committed the perfect crime. And that *you* are the only connecting link between two inexplicable deaths. Try as I'd like to, I can't escape that fact. It wouldn't strain credulity to believe that you, Du Pont and Nelson were in this together. I don't say I believe that. But I have to examine the possibility, don't I, to do *my* job?"

"I guess you do," the lawyer said with some emphasis, and went back to sit down behind his desk. "Just remember, I didn't know Nelson until after I came back from Europe. You can check that with Lawrence Emerson."

"I'll be running along." Fernandez went to the door. "ESP! Jesus!" He shook his head with disgust and left.

Ralston felt heavy and tired. He sat at his desk for a long time after Fernandez left, doing nothing, unable to think, but unable to forget. He flicked the intercom switch eventually.

"Marcia, can Mr. Reikert see me?"

"Yes, Mr. Ralston," she said after a pause.

"I'll be right up."

"Yessir."

Ralston told his own secretary that he would be with the senior partner for about half an hour. Reikert listened sympathetically and readily agreed to Ralston's taking time off; there would be no problem redistributing his case load. When he left Reikert's office, Ralston felt as though a great burden had been lifted from his shoulders.

On the way home he stopped by a travel agent's and picked up all the brochures they had on the Far East.

Anticipating the coming month was sheer joy. Ralston felt twenty years younger. He was suddenly burning with enthusiasm and a sense of adventure. From the very moment he had spread the travel brochures on the dinner table in front of Carol, the trip had dominated their every thought. There was much hurried organizing, since he intended to waste not a moment before leaving; last-minute arrangements, planning, and evaluating the course of their trip. Instead of "doing" the Far East in one month, they decided to concentrate on a few, carefully selected places. With characteristic thoroughness, Ralston sifted through each and every possibility, finally settling on the four most interesting and appealing places. He researched each stop so that he knew exactly what to see and how to see it. There was no detail he overlooked.

By the evening before they took off, they were all ready, packed, organized, and eager to go. Some friends had wanted to give them a going-away party, but the Ralstons decided to do that themselves, so they could simply go upstairs and to bed when it was over. Just as the house was filling with guests, the telephone rang.

"I'm terribly sorry to bother you, Cary," Nelson said. "But something has come up. I'd like to take some special filtered photos of the original book. I won't have another chance."

"Sure. Come over when you want." Ralston couldn't help the old curiosity from welling up again. Even in the face of the trip, he found himself unable to contain it. "What's up?"

"Can I tell you when I get there? It's a little complicated and I've got some things to do before I come over."

"Sure."

When Nelson arrived, Ralston quietly slipped away with him down to the cellar. "What's going on?"

"On one of the Xerox copies, we thought there was a faint impression of something that might have been written in the margin. If I photograph the originals with these filters I've brought, I hope we'll be able to read it."

"You can even develop them here. I have a full setup."

"Good."

"Have you got anywhere with the translation?"

"No. Although this language looks like Arabic, it has no relation to it, at least, as far as we know."

"You think this marginal writing could help?"

"I pray it will. The smallest clue could be the crack in the dam."

Ralston led the professor to the book, which he had taken down to the cellar after the call. Nelson took out the Xerox copy and compared it with several pages as he carefully turned them.

"This is it." Nelson began taking several photos, changing the filters after four or five shots. "If this doesn't work, would you allow us to treat the page chemically?"

"It depends. Those pages are pretty weak. I coated them, you know."

"Yes, well, I can assure you we'd check with you before trying anything. We could test the chemicals on the corners of various pages first. But, let's not jump to that. First, we ought to see if these filters bring it out. This is a special camera. They ought to."

Ralston showed the professor over to the photographic equipment in the corner. Ralston had about everything required. Nelson ran the films through the baths and hung them up to dry.

"There's a bit more. Markham called me this morning. Last night he was working on his notes, when of a sudden his hand started writing—without his willing it. In the language of this book."

Ralston squinted incredulously, "Oh, come on."

"I know it sounds crazy. But Markham is not one to make wild statements."

"He could have copied it, or remembered it. Subconsciously."

"I've looked at the writing. Whatever it is it certainly looks like the language of our book, but as far as I can see, it is not one of the passages *from* the book. You may ask how I can be so sure since I can't read the language? Just from the variations and combinations of the symbols. But I could be mistaken."

"I think we are all getting slightly obsessed with this thing."

"You could be right. I don't know why I feel such a compulsion to get the book translated. Anyway, Markham also had some other news. He thinks he's beginning to break the symbol code." Nelson said it with a far-off look.

"Really?" Ralston felt the old excitement again.

"He's having a meeting tonight with two other professors, from the physics and astronomy departments."

"Why?"

Nelson replied with slight pique. "Why ask me? I'm not privy to what Markham is doing. In any case, this week he is bringing his notes and we are going to check it out on the computer."

"Do you think it'll help translate the language?"

"It could. If we find out what the symbols mean, we might assume the language related to it somehow. And if we know what the language is talking *about,* it might give us some idea of what each particular sentence or word means. On the other hand, it might not help at all."

"Cary, are you down there?" It was Carol's voice calling from the top of the cellar stairs.

"Yes, Darling. I'll be up in a minute."

"We do have guests, Sweetheart."

"In a minute."

"Okay." They could hear the door shut above them.

"I don't want to keep you away from your party. I can finish up here."

"That's all right. I'd like to see what turns up."

They moved back to the films. They were dry enough to

make the prints. Just when they were beginning to give up hope, something started to come up on one of them. "Look," Nelson said.

"Don't leave it in too long," Ralston cautioned. The sense of excitement made them both tingle.

"Here it comes. Here it comes." He took the print out of the bath and hung it up to dry.

"Can you read it?"

"Have you got a magnifying glass?"

Ralston fetched one and gave it to Nelson. The professor scanned the dripping print.

"What does it say?" Ralston leaned forward with undisguised intensity.

"It's Latin. Yes. No, here, this is a French word. It says something like 'The source. Basis of all grimoires. The fundamental knowledge . . .' and then it fades off again. Perhaps there isn't any more."

"What does it mean?"

"Have you got a French dictionary down here?"

"Yes," Ralston said, stepping toward the bookshelves. He took down the dictionary and handed it to Nelson.

The professor scanned the pages. "Ah, 'grimoire'. Let's see. 'A black book. A book of magic. A wizard's book.' " Nelson looked up. "It matches up with those notes, all right. You said the baron was a scholar, didn't you?"

"Yes."

"My guess is that he wrote this . . . and the notes. If he could understand the book, there's no reason we shouldn't too." Nelson seemed to drift away on the thought.

"If it's only some old magic book, is it worth it?"

"Magic? Or science? The note says this is the *source* of grimoires, not that it *is* a grimoire. If you put that together with what Markham thinks he's found . . ."

There was a pause until Ralston asked, "It means what?"

114

"It means this could be the source of your Necronomicon and all the rest." Nelson paused. "I ought to tell you. I did some research on the Necronomicon. It was the invention of a writer, H. P. Lovecraft. The interesting thing about him is that he dreamed everything he wrote. Wild dreams."

"He could have been on drugs like Poe."

"No. He claimed not. Anyway, the Necronomicon is fictitious. Then why did whoever read this book of ours mention it? Your baron must have thought there was some connection. Why would he think this the source of a fictitious book? Unless there actually was a Necronomicon."

"You think this writer's dreams could have been something more? Like a revelation?"

"No." Nelson sounded sure. Then his mind seemed to seize on something else. "Perhaps what is meant is that this book is the source of real and fictional magic books. After all, any book of magic is fiction. There is no magic. The question is whether this is just another fictional work," he said, tapping the book, "or whether it is some kind of scientific knowledge mistaken for magic. Whatever it is, we have to find out the answer, don't we?"

"Maybe we're opening Pandora's Box."

"Maybe. The men who invented the atomic bomb had the same worries. Was the world ready for the knowledge and all that. My view is that science must seek the truth. If man chooses to pervert knowledge, that is his mistake. But science can neither hide the truth nor hide from it. We have an obligation. It's the same as translating these dead languages. Some would say it is a waste of time, that we ought to be spending our money and energy on more practical things, like cleaning up pollution, but I don't think so. We must search out anything that adds to the corpus of human knowledge because knowledge, of all kinds, is the answer to our problems. History is relevant. We learn from the mistakes of others. The history of science is very relevant. Pandora's Box? No. Knowledge itself is neither good nor bad. It is only what man does with it that makes it good or bad."

"Well, I agree with you. I didn't mean seriously that we ought to burn the thing, you know. It's just that I have an odd feeling, as if we were standing on a threshold."

"Yes, Cary. That's just what we are doing. When we walk through the doors, we may find nothing of note, or we might find out that some ancient race knew as much about higher mathematics as we do now. That would mean revising a lot of ideas and getting closer to the truth. If Markham is right, we might rewrite quite a bit of history when we're finished."

CHAPTER SEVEN

◎

The moment they set foot on the airplane, all thoughts of the mainland slipped away. The break was physical and spiritual. For three days they lounged around the hotel in Honolulu, and Ralston's only thoughts were whether to get up for another "Hawaii Kai" or go back into the sun. The warm, balmy air was like a pillow; his mind was empty and he simply floated in pleasure. Carol too could not have been happier. They were really together again for the first time since their honeymoon. She remembered the old saw, "The law is a jealous mistress" and for the first time she understood its full import. Being totally with her husband, making pleasant decisions the whole day about things they both wanted to do, Cary's physical presence, was all a luxury she knew she would miss when it was over. The island was a perfumed paradise of exotic smells and caressing climate. By the time the three days had gone by, they were both rested for the adventures their trip was to hold.

When they left the island, Cary Ralston's worst worry was a painful sunburn. His skin had been unprepared for the burning hot sun of Hawaii. He smelled of Coppertone, but even with the liberal applications his shoulders seemed to crinkle every time he moved and he had the impression that sand had somehow worked up under his suit.

From the moment they landed in Singapore, Carol was a whirlwind of activity, racing from bazaar to shop, picking through everything in the sidewalk vendors' carts, determined to find a bargain in the form of a precious gem (she had heard stories of tourists to whom fabulous gems had been brought from the most implausible sources—forgetting, unfortunately, that the stories tended to be somewhat dated, if not embellished). At the end of each day they returned to their hotel exhausted, their feet aching, but only to bathe and dress and then go out again for an adventurous evening. They also managed to cram in all that Ralston wanted to see; if it was physically tiring, it was mentally rejuvenating. They took a three-day excursion to Kuala Lumpur, which proved interesting, if not quite as exotic as anticipated or as comfortable as hoped. Then they flew off to Taipei for a few days, to get away from the touristy places. From there they went to Hong Kong for a week. Once again, Carol found the shops irresistible. They saw the sights, what there was of them, had a quick long-distance view of Red China, and ate on floating restaurants. And finally, they went to Tokyo and Osaka, with a couple of days spent roving around the countryside by car. Japan was a highlight, if only because they both adored sashimi and gorged themselves shamelessly for days. They spent a month of sheer pleasure, never once thinking about home, or even of returning, and when they finally boarded the flight back to Hawaii, it was with sadness and regret that they could not have stayed longer. But at least they had something to look forward to—a few days' rest at the Hana Maui. It was a superb experience, well planned for rest and diversion, and when they got back to

Los Angeles Ralston was a new man and Carol felt years younger. They vowed it would never be so long before they traveled again.

They arrived back on a Sunday and the house looked strange to them. There was a pile of mail on the hall table. Most of it was bills. There were letters from out-of-town friends. And an intriguing postcard from Nelson. "Call. I think I have something to tell you." It was postmarked during the first week of their trip. Ralston telephoned but there was no answer.

Monday morning they woke to a perfect day. The sun was bright. There wasn't a trace of smog and the whole of Los Angeles shimmered in brilliant light. Ralston edged the Mercedes out along Sunset, cut through Brentwood to San Vicente, and eventually found his way to Wilshire, which bore him to the office. Things seemed momentarily strange, though he knew nothing had changed: the receptionist still wore the same smile, geared to catch some wealthy client, she hoped. His secretary was her usual efficient self. He went up to see Reikert and the rest. They were happy to see him back but happier to get back to their own problems. No one was interested in hearing about his trip. He wandered back down to his own office and before starting on the day's business, decided to try to reach Nelson again.

"Oh, Betty, would you get me Professor Nelson at UCLA when you get back to your desk?" She looked at him with a curious expression on her face.

"Nelson?"

"Yes, why?"

"I don't know if it's the same one . . ."

"The same one as what?"

"Sir, I think a Professor Nelson was murdered at UCLA,

along with three others, about three weeks ago. Soon after you left."

"What?"

"It was in all the papers, but I guess you wouldn't have read about it. Of course, this might be a different Professor Nelson . . ."

"What happened? Do you know?"

"That's why I remember it. It was supposed to be really gruesome. In fact, the papers didn't print any of the details. But you know the to-do. It was like the Manson thing again."

Ralston's voice rasped, "Get me Captain Robert Fernandez at the LAPD Central Division."

"I'm sorry, Mr. Ralston. I didn't mean to upset you."

"It's all right. Just get me Fernandez."

Still apologetic, his secretary backed out to her own office. All the peace and relaxation of the trip faded away. Ralston's hands were trembling. He took off his jacket and hung it up and lurched at the telephone when it rang.

"Christ Almighty," Fernandez said with urgency, "when did you get back?"

"Yesterday. Bob . . ."

"You've heard."

"I've got to talk to you."

"Not on the phone. I'm coming up that way this morning. I can see you in an hour or so."

Waiting for Fernandez, Ralston paced his office, unable to be still. He desperately wanted to have more information but knew that his best source would be there soon enough. Finally, he went over to the window and pulled up the venetian blinds. It couldn't have been more beautiful. The sky was bright blue, the hills were sharply etched, and Beverly Hills looked like a dream of tomorrow. It simply was not the kind of place where such strange things happened. These mysteries were better set in the brooding dank English countryside, or along the storm-racked lakes of Switzerland, but not in the bright, ultra-modern splendor of Southern California, the land of the future. It just didn't fit, and yet it was happening. He remembered what Greenberg had said, that he was afraid to face the possibility of the supernatural, and yet he knew that that was exactly what he would have to face after he saw Fernandez. There was little doubt in Ralston's mind that the murders were another horrifying and insoluble enigma.

The minutes dragged by, each one taking an eternity. The unreality of the affair weighed on him. He did not have to be told who the other victims were—Markham, a professor of astronomy and a professor of physics. The whole thing was incredible. It was all too incredible.

Fernandez arrived, looking drawn and tired. He shut the door behind him. His manner was apologetic, sympathetic. "Cary."

"Bob, what happened?"

"Much the same thing as happened to Ferguesson."

"Oh, my God." Ralston sank down in his chair. "How?"

Fernandez tried to tell it without emotion, but he could not hide the immensity of his shock. "They'd been working at night. One of the assistants, a student, went out for coffee. When he came back, the door was locked. He heard what went on inside." Fernandez stopped, trying to find the right words.

"What happened inside?"

"Sounds. Sounds like he had never heard before. Sounds of four men being torn to pieces, I suppose you could say. He called the police. When we arrived, the door was still locked. Have you been to Nelson's lab?"

"Yes."

"Then you know there aren't any windows. The whole thing's underground and air-conditioned for the computer."

"Yes, I know," Ralston mumbled.

"We had to break down the door. There was nothing there . . . except them . . . or what was left of them. They were ripped to pieces. One was clawed up, the coroner says."

"The heads . . . ?" Ralston began.

"Missing."

They both sat without speaking while Ralston tried to sort it out in his mind. Fernandez' head sunk heavily on his chest. "Cary, I have to ask you this. Where were you on the twenty-second?"

Ralston looked up slowly, the realization of what Fernandez meant not quickly coming to mind. "The twenty-second?" He didn't seem able to concentrate. "Oh, yes," he said dreamily, "we were in Singapore, I think. I can check."

"You'll have to."

Ralston glanced over to Fernandez. "I wasn't in the country."

"Okay. Okay. But we'll have to have proof. Understand?"

"Yes," Ralston replied drearily. His mind was spinning and his head throbbed.

"All this happened in the space of minutes. The student thinks he heard it all."

"In minutes?"

They sat in abject silence again, not looking at each other, but through each other. "Cary, can you tell me anything? Anything at all?"

"I don't think so. Nothing you would think reasonable. You just wouldn't believe it."

"Try me. Is there anything, anything at all, that could

be a link between these murders?" Fernandez sounded desperate, almost pleading.

"Just one. I've thought about it over and over and as crazy as it sounds, it's the only common denominator. Still, I just don't see how it could really have anything to do with all this. The book."

"What book?"

"I told you, when I was in France, I went to an auction of the baron's library. I bought several items and amongst them was one large book. I didn't know what it was. I met Nelson and thought he might be able to help. I asked him to take a look at it. Nelson called in Markham and Markham called in the others."

"How did Ferguesson figure in all this?"

"He didn't . . ." Ralston weighed the possibilities. ". . . except he knew Nelson."

"What book is this?" Fernandez asked.

"I have it at home. I can show you. It's a very old book, written in some forgotten language. Nelson was trying to translate it."

"Had he?"

"No. But the book was divided into written language and some kind of symbols. Markham thought the symbols might be mathematical formulas."

"Or something to do with astronomy or physics?"

"Yes."

"And your baron once owned the book. All right, it's a connection. They all had something to do with the book, except possibly Ferguesson. But where does this get us?" Fernandez was too weary to play intellectual games.

"Let me finish," Ralston begged. He wanted to unload everything and have someone else share the burden. "Nelson . . . and I suppose Markham . . . thought the book was a record of highly advanced concepts. It might show that some ancient cult knew as much about things as we did . . . or even more. Can you go along with that?"

"I'm just listening, Cary. I'm still trying to figure what your point is."

"All right. Nelson said a book of science . . . if it was a book of science . . . might be mistaken for magic. In other words, my book could be a magic book . . . what they call a grimoire . . . or it might have hidden scientific ideas."

"If you're trying to tell me that they were killed by magic, I think we'd better have a little chat with your friend Greenberg. Or is that why you went there?"

"I am telling you the facts. I am telling you what Markham and Nelson believed. I am not talking about magic. I am talking about knowledge hidden in that book which perhaps they discovered and which killed them."

"An experiment gone wrong?"

"It's possible. Let's say Markham had come up with something and they tried to implement what was in the book . . . and . . ."

"And? First, what tore them to pieces? Whatever it was wasn't there when we arrived."

"Some sort of force field, I don't know."

"Now you're a physicist. Fine. Okay, maybe they created some sort of power or explosion. We don't know. I could almost go along with that, but it's straight from science fiction. It still doesn't explain Ferguesson."

"Not really."

"I think you're putting me on."

"Bob, I don't know if that book has anything to do with all this. I only know that it *is* the only common factor. I've told you what everyone was working on. You take it from there. Now you know everything I do."

Fernandez folded his hands on his lap and interlaced the fingers. "The whole case is crazy and so's everyone involved. I'm beginning to think someone dumped LSD in the city water supply and we've all been on a trip. A bad trip." He started rubbing his eyes. "I'm a simple cop. A plain, dumb, honest flatfoot. I read though. When it comes to a midnight bull session about the Martians, I can hold my own. But Goddamn it!" he said very loudly, "this is a murder investigation, not the Late, Late Show."

Fernandez lit a cigarette and started pacing in front of Ralston's desk. "For Heaven's sake, tell me you're not serious."

Ralston stared past the policeman, into space. "I wish I could." He buried his face in his hands. "God help me."

Fernandez sat down heavily again. "You must believe it or you wouldn't be telling me. I just can't believe it. It's way over my head. Sorry, if I yelled."

"Forget it."

"Okay, the book is a common link. Maybe I have to look into the damned thing after all. I'll start with the tapes."

Ralston's head came up slowly. "What tapes?"

"Nelson put his notes on tape."

Ralston spoke with resolution. "I don't know what's the matter with me. For Christ's sake, if there's a problem, let's face it and to hell with it. There's no point running around with my tail between my legs. Can I listen to the tapes with you?"

"Why not?"

"Okay. I'd like to have a look around Nelson's office and the lab. As a matter of fact, I'd like to look over the offices of the other professors."

"Why?"

"Because I might see something that ties in."

"We've been over all those places with a fine-toothed comb. What do you think you can find that we can't?"

"I don't know. I won't know until I look."

Fernandez thought a moment. "If this whole thing wasn't so damned odd, I'd say no."

"Good, now let me ask you a couple of questions. Is there any chance that some piece of equipment in the lab could have caused the injuries?"

Fernandez shot him a pained look. "No. Don't you think we checked that immediately?"

"Okay then, what about your idea that there could have been some secret research going on out there?"

"Not according to the university."

"They wouldn't tell you if it was classified."

"I've already requested complete clearance from the Federal government. Satisfied?" he said, sarcastically.

"Okay. I'm just asking." Ralston drummed his fingers. "What about the student? Can you tell me exactly what he said?"

"Right. This kid was working on another project, something that Nelson was supervising. He was in the lab and went out for coffee. He remembers they seemed excited about something just before he left. He walked down to the cafeteria and had coffee and something to eat, then walked back. He was gone about forty minutes. When he got back, the door was locked. He knocked. He heard screams from inside. To use his own words, it sounded like an elephant was in the lab. Then he heard this . . ." Fernandez glanced up, as if forcing the word out ". . . this slurping sound. Mind you, the doors to the lab are pretty thick. Sound would be distorted. Then he telephoned the police."

"Anything else?"

"The smell. The officers who first arrived on the scene

broke the door down. The first thing they noticed was an offensive smell."

"Did they describe it?"

"They said it was horrible, that's all. Oh, wait, I think one of them said it was something like decayed garbage. But you must know, Cary, when a man's belly is ripped open, it smells pretty foul. There were the contents of four ripped bellies strewn all over that lab. It still stank when I got there, rancid, and a little sour." He blenched at the memory.

"What about notes?"

"We've collected everything each of the victims was working on and an expert in each department is going over them. Of course, we didn't know anything about this book. I'll have to mention it . . . somehow." Fernandez was wondering how he could broach the subject to the professors without sounding as crazy as Ralston. "And one of Nelson's chief assistants is working on the tapes. Whitney."

"Would you mind if I talked to Whitney?"

"I really don't think you ought to poke around too much. After all . . ."

"After all, I might come up with something. You never know."

"From what I've seen, Nelson's work was pretty complicated. I don't think you have the expertise necessary. Neither do I. I'll tell you what, after Whitney is finished going over the notes, you can talk to him. I don't want you disturbing him now."

Ralston's disappointment needed no vocal expression.

Fernandez felt a little guilty. "I wouldn't like to find you splattered around some room, Cary." Fernandez waved his hand as if he was trying to erase that remark. "It's not that I don't appreciate your trying to help. I do. But this is a particularly nasty matter. It's not for amateurs. Excuse me for putting it so bluntly. But you and I were in the army, right? We don't give advice to generals now. So even if you were a D.A. a few years ago, you're a civilian now."

"But I *am* involved."

"No more. You leave this to the experts. I promise you, I'll check into what you've said. But now you stop."

"You still don't think there's a connection through the book."

"Honestly, I don't. Don't you understand how incredible it sounds? Magic or lost scientific secrets! I really think it's best you leave it alone, Cary. We don't know what we're dealing with. There could be a homicidal maniac running around. He may have some tool or device we don't yet know about. But whoever he is or whatever it is, it's close enough to you. And stop thinking up these wild theories or you'll find yourself really sick."

Fernandez left, shaking his head. He really had come close to thinking Ralston had cracked up. The story was so wild that he could come to no other conclusion. And that led him to an even more painful thought: a man as mad as Cary Ralston appeared to be could commit such crimes. But after checking with Singapore, he had to abandon this idea. The Singapore police had records of all incoming and outgoing travelers; Ralston had arrived on the nineteenth and did not leave until the twenty-sixth. It was physically impossible for him to be in Los Angeles on the twenty-second, the date of the murders. It had also been proved that he was not in France at the time the baron was murdered. Of course, there remained the possibility that Ralston worked with a confederate—but if he was insane, that was highly unlikely. Homicidal maniacs did not work in teams.

Fernandez was at the end of his tether. He had no explanation for any of the occurrences. Nor had the French Sûreté come up with any theory either. Both police departments were completely baffled.

Ralston was shattered over Nelson's death. He was sure the book had something to do with it, and it was he who had put Nelson in danger by asking his advice and help in translating. Fernandez, a man whom he had once respected and been respected by in return, thought him quite mad. Even Dr. Greenberg had made some allusion to it, hadn't he? Wasn't Ralston overtired? Didn't he need a rest? Ralston could not face the situation alone. There was no Nelson to confide in now and Emerson would only scoff at him. The only person to whom he could turn was Carol, but would he be exposing her to danger? The problem was that she could not be put off too much longer. Carol was no fool. Sooner or later she would tumble to the whole thing. And worse, he needed her. He needed her levelheaded advice, her confidence in him, and her knowledge of him. Surely she would know whether or not he was mad.

After dinner, they went into the study. He was debating how he could broach the subject when she removed the option of any choice. "Darling, did you know that your friend Professor Nelson had an accident?" She was breaking it as gently as she thought she could.

"Yes. He's dead."

"Then you know. I wonder why you didn't mention it to me?"

"Perhaps it slipped my mind."

"I don't think something like that would, Cary. And you must have heard it today. Why didn't you tell me?"

"Carol, you know the professor and I were working on something . . ."

"Translating that old book."

"All right. But it's not that simple."

"I've known that for a long time, Darling. I was hoping you would finally tell me."

"It's not that I wanted to keep anything from you, but Carol, suppose there was danger?"

Her frown heightened the look of surprise on her face. "Danger?" She thought only a moment before saying, "Then I think we ought to share it."

"I don't know. I don't know if I can risk your life."

She came over to him and took his hand. "Cary, you are my life. I wouldn't have anything without you. Don't interrupt, please. I know it sounds a little old-fashioned, but I really love you. I always have and I always will. There could never be anyone like you again, not for me. I'd rather take my chances with you."

"Come here," he said, pulling her down and kissing her. "Now, how about the mystery?"

"I hope to God I'm doing the right thing."

"You are. Tell me. I've known something was bothering you. You've been so preoccupied, except on the trip."

"I got away from things."

"What things? Come on, Cary, don't make me pull it out inch by inch."

He told her. He set it all down in chronological order. He tried only to relate the facts, just as he'd done with Fernandez. When he was finished, she sat there with a confused and worried expression on her face.

"I think you're right. It has to be the book. What else can it be? But it's so impossible."

"I know. Darling, do you think I'm nuts?"

"Is that what's bothering you? No, of course not."

"I can't vouch for all the facts. I got it hearsay from Du Pont and he had it hearsay too. But Fernandez spoke with the Paris police. I can't be sure he's told me everything but I think he has, substantially. I talked to Nelson myself. Well, that's it."

"What do you want to do, Darling? I mean, you can't translate the book. You don't know anything about that."

"No, but Whitney does. That's Nelson's assistant. Fernandez has him going over Nelson's notes on tape."

She mulled it over for a minute. "If Nelson was killed, Cary, and all the others . . ."

"Should I leave it alone?"

"Yes. They were all experts."

"I wonder. Maybe we need an expert in something else."

"In what?"

"Isn't there some university where they work on this type of thing?" Ralston searched his memory. "I seem to remember Nelson mentioning something."

"Cary, you know I'm not superstitious or anything, but maybe it's best if we don't find out. Maybe you ought to leave it alone. Or at least turn it over to someone else."

"Nelson said there was a duty to find out."

"But look what happened to him. He was killed."

"Yes, I know. And I blame myself for that partly."

"You shouldn't. He knew as much about it as you do, maybe more. But don't you think there are things that are better left alone?"

"Honestly, Carol, I don't know. Yes, I think so, and no, I don't."

"If you want to go on then, let's talk about it. What's the best way?"

"Like you say, I'll never be able to translate the thing. I certainly don't know enough about math to get as far as Markham either. On both counts, I lose. I could put it to people at the university, I suppose, but they'd probably think I was out of my mind."

"And they might end up just the way Nelson and the others did. So might you. Darling, this scares me."

"It scares me too, but that's because we don't understand it. I do have a logical mind, even if it's a little shaken at the moment."

"Then leave it alone until you feel ready. Don't press it until you can cope with it. Wait until you know what's right."

"That makes sense. I promise you."

"And promise me that if you do anything more about it, you'll tell me."

"Okay," he said reluctantly.

"Promise."

"I promise." Ralston felt more relieved now that Carol knew. He also felt more confident because she did not discount the possibility of what he was thinking: Okay, if you are going to go into a problem, then you have to do some research. At least, to begin with, I can read up on some of the things Nelson was talking about. I can find out if there are experts in this sort of thing. And I can find out what Whitney knows.

Barnard Whitney, Associate Professor of Languages, lived in the same confusion of books as had Nelson. His office was a mad disarray of books and papers piled in the most haphazard fashion. Whitney himself was just as messy; he had a shock of black, unkempt hair, a sallow complexion, and one of the lenses of his rimless eyeglasses had a tiny crack in the upper edge. A cigarette dangled from his lips and the smoke drifted up into his blinking eyes.

"Dr. Whitney?"

"Sit down," he said peremptorily. "Sit down, Mr. Rawlings."

"Ralston."

"Yes, yes." He removed his glasses and turned to face his visitor. "What can I do for you?"

Ralston proffered his card.

"Dear me, am I being sued?"

"Nothing like that."

"I can't imagine why anyone would want to sue me."

"No one does, as far as I know. I'd like to talk to you about Professor Nelson."

Whitney's face darkened. "Tragic. Tragic case. Do you represent the estate?"

"No. Dr. Whitney, Professor Nelson and I were working on something together. I have reason to believe he was working on it the night he was killed, and so were Markham and the others."

"Ah . . . hum. Ralston, yes."

"Then you know what I'm talking about."

"Yes. Yes, indeed, but I can't talk to you about it, I'm afraid."

"Why not?"

"Confidential. You'd have to clear it with the police."

"Oh, I see. So Fernandez has told you not to talk to me. I'm afraid he can't do that, Doctor."

"No?"

"No. And besides, since Nelson was working on my book in a joint project, I have a right to whatever findings he had." Ralston waited to let that sink in, then added, "It wouldn't be difficult to get a court order."

"You know more about the law than I do, Mr. Rawlings."

"Ralston."

"But I really ought not."

"I already know a good deal about it."

"I don't suppose there's any harm in telling you this

133

much. Professor Nelson was a very brilliant man. I'm hardly in his league. It would take me years to get as far as he did. I've listened to his notes and I really can't make much out of them. Nelson had his own shorthand . . . and put that on top of your book, and I very much fear the thing is far too complicated to solve. I've told as much to Captain Fernandez. I will work on it a little more."

"I ought to warn you. Professor Nelson thought the book might be a grimoire."

Whitney laughed. "I hardly think that's likely."

"Let me put it this way. He thought it might contain knowledge of math or science which could have been mistaken for a grimoire."

"That's possible, of course."

"And that's why he asked Professor Markham to work on the symbols."

"You seem to know a great deal about this."

"I told you. I was working with them."

"I knew Professor Nelson quite well, Mr. Rawlings. I can assure you that if he had any interest in this at all, it was solely to translate an unknown tongue, for whatever information it contained."

"And something they found out killed them."

"I really doubt that."

"I am only warning you because I don't think you understand the full implications of what you are getting into."

"That's very good of you. But I assure you, there are no grimoires. If, as you say, there is scientific knowledge contained in the book, what harm can there be in that?"

"I really don't know. I only know that various people who have had a connection with the book have died horribly and inexplicably. I've always believed that where there's smoke, there's fire."

"I will agree to this, Mr. Rawlings, that if you can get

a court order, I will tell you whatever I find out. But for the moment, I certainly cannot go against the orders of the police. I can say that as of now I know very little, perhaps not even as much as you."

"Then I'll get that court order. Do you mind if I ask you a couple of questions?"

"If they do not require an answer which I have been requested not to give."

"All right. If I wanted to learn something about your field, could you suggest a couple of texts?"

"I don't see any harm in that. Yes, Dedrickson, by all means." He turned toward his shelves and took down a large volume. "Can't lend you mine. Sorry. Need it. You might find it somewhere though. There's not much call for it normally. And you could look at Von Kerdler, the Williamson translation."

Ralston wrote down the names of the books. "One more thing. If I wanted to look into grimoires—things like that—can you suggest any books, or could you suggest someone who is an expert in the field?"

"I suppose you are talking about the occult?"

"I don't know. Am I?"

"Black magic, that sort of thing? I don't know much about it. There are undoubtedly many books. As to experts, I can only think of the Parapsychology Unit at Duke University. As far as I know, they study various phenomena, but mainly ESP and related subjects. That's Dr. Rhine. He gave a talk here at UCLA once. I'm afraid that's all I can do for you."

"It helps. Can you tell me if all the notes were on the tape?"

"I don't know if I can tell you that."

"Well, I think you can. Do you know if Markham kept notes of his own?"

"Not about this. Several people went through his records; they had nothing to do with this. The only notes I know about were Nelson's tapes."

"Are you planning to get help in working on the notes?"

"Not at the moment, no."

"Would you consider working with me once I have a court order?"

"On the book? You mean actually translating it? I don't see that I will have the time. After all, Professor Nelson's death has left us very short-staffed. We have a huge backlog of work. And I'm afraid I really don't have that compelling an interest in your project, at the moment, and I am working on a book of my own. My time is very limited just now."

"I quite understand."

"I think I've already said too much."

Ralston left Whitney buried once more in his books. But just before he went out, he caught a glimpse of one title lying open on the desk: *Imhotep: Myth or Genius?*

CHAPTER EIGHT

◎

The corridors of the Central Police building were busy, with a motley of police officers and scraggy youths, criminals, and victims. Far removed from the confusion of the floors below, Robert M. Fernandez, Jr., Captain, Homicide Division, looked out over the yellow-brown smog hovering over City Hall. Standing in front of him was Denton Arvey Speke, Assistant District Attorney. Speke was a big man who looked like a football player rather than a lawyer—and indeed, he had been first-string end at USC. He was ruggedly handsome and thought of by most as a comer. But comers liked to make things happen and for that reason, Fernandez always dreaded having Speke assigned to one of his cases. Speke was a bulldog who never let go. He pushed hard. He wanted results.

"It's been damned near six months," he said, rather too harshly.

"I know it," Fernandez said with a trace of irritation.

"What have you turned up? Nothing. I'm getting flak from the D.A."

Fernandez didn't really believe that. Only Speke wanted to crack these cases. It would have been a real feather in his cap. "We're still digging, but frankly, we haven't found

137

much. We've interviewed the students. We've been over the life histories of Nelson, Ralston, Markham and the others. The French police have done the same with both Mr. and Mrs. du Pont and the Baron de Chantille. They haven't come up with anything. About the only thing we do know is that almost anybody Ferguesson dealt with had a reason to kill him. On the basis of motive I figure we have about three hundred suspects. There are only two links—the MO of the murders, and a book six people were connected with in one way or another. But what that shows, I can't say."

"Bob, this kind of thing doesn't look too good. I've got people on my back. I've even heard one of the papers is planning an exposé."

"The papers won't get anything."

"Don't be too sure. There's always someone who'll sell out for enough money. What about this MO?"

"What about it? We've covered every angle. If you can explain how it was done, be my guest. We've contacted practically every forensic lab in the Western world and no one has the remotest idea."

"We've got to get a break."

"Well, sir, what do you suggest?"

"I don't know. Listen, Bob, we're both rational men. There has to be an explanation."

"That's what I keep telling myself. Look, I've even had clearance to run over every secret project the government has. There's not a thing that could do this."

"You're really sure the government is telling you everything?"

"No, of course not. But I tell you the experts can't even come up with a wild theory that fits the circumstances."

The two men chewed over the facts again without coming to any conclusion and finally Speke asked Marshall and Lynden at the lab to come up.

"Can you describe the murders in nontechnical terms?" Speke said.

Marshall did. "Ferguesson and the four professors were literally torn limb from limb, right down to their fingers. They were nothing but bits and pieces when we found them. We know, in the case of the professors, that all this happened in something like ten minutes. There was no piece of equipment in the lab which could have caused it."

"What about something that exploded and was used up?" Speke said.

"Not consistent with the injuries. Lab analysis of the walls and floors turned up nothing. There was no chemical residue of any kind. In any case, there was certainly nothing in Ferguesson's house remotely connected with the lab. The French analysts came up with substantially the same thing."

"My God, man," Speke sputtered, "there has to be some explanation."

Marshall looked at Fernandez and shrugged.

"If there is, I can't think of it."

"Nor I," Lynden said, shaking his head.

"What about a maniac . . . or even a group of maniacs?" Speke insisted.

"One, how did they get in and out of the lab? Two, how did they do it? Okay, let's say they had some machine that could pull a man to pieces. The problem is that the pathology shows it happened quickly. For example, had it happened slowly, the victim would have been dead long before every piece of him was pulled apart, and would have stopped bleeding. But each part showed bleeding concurrently."

"All right, thanks," Speke said. After they left, he sat down again and hung a massive leg over the arm of the chair. "What do we do?"

"I'm at a dead end," Fernandez said, swiveling around to face the Assistant D.A.

"Aren't you planning to do anything at all?"

"I've got a man working on translating that book. But he's not quite the man Nelson was. He works very slowly."

"What's the book got to do with it?"

"I don't know. It's a common factor, that's all."

"What good will it do to translate it?"

"I won't know that until it *is* translated."

"Bah, it's a waste of time."

"It may be but it's all we have."

"Can't you prod this fellow a little?"

"I can try," Fernandez said with resignation. "I'll go out there today."

Speke didn't say anything for a while. "It has to be some new weapon."

"If it is, I don't know how we are going to find out about it."

"Maybe we can put some pressure on through political circles."

"You're welcome to try."

"Of course, you know, it might not be ours."

Fernandez lifted an eyebrow. "Maybe not." The idea was too ridiculous to consider, but it was not more so than the whole case. When Speke left, Fernandez heaved a sigh of relief. Speke would never let go, but the police captain had learned something in all his years in office—how to accept the unanswerable. There had been other cases which he had not been able to solve. Sooner or later, you forgot about them.

As he had promised, Fernandez went out to the university after lunch. It was a great pleasure to get away from the office for a while. He took the Harbor Freeway to the Santa Monica Freeway, then up the San Diego Freeway, and reached the UCLA campus in about half an hour.

"Dr. Whitney has not been in since last Wednesday." The girl at the Humanities Office desk told him. "We've tried to call him several times."

"Is that unusual?"

"No. We're in the middle of finals. He has no classes."

"Let me have his address, will you?"

"I'm sorry, we don't give out that information." When Fernandez showed his credentials, the girl relented with goggled eyes.

Fernandez drove out to Sherman Oaks, in the Valley, to Whitney's house. It was a modest, one-story structure on a pleasant street. He rang the doorbell. There was no answer. He walked around the side of the house and peered in the windows. It was too dark for him to see anything. Finally, he tried the rear door but it was locked. There were several milk bottles on the back stoop. Fernandez decided to try the house next door. A woman answered his ring; she was about thirty, pleasant-looking, with her hair wrapped in a towel. He showed her his badge and she opened the door.

"Is something wrong?"

"Perhaps you can tell me. Do you know Dr. Whitney next door?"

"Oh, yes. Has something happened to him?"

"Why do you ask?"

She shrugged. "I don't think he's home."

"When was the last time you saw him, Ma'am?"

"Well, it must be a couple of weeks. But I did see his lights on last Friday, I think it was."

"You didn't see him over the weekend?"

She thought a minute. "No."

"Would you normally see him? I mean does he garden or sunbathe . . . ?"

"No. I mean, we don't see him that much, just to say hello. But you know when someone's there or not, don't you?"

"Would you say it was odd if you didn't see him for five or six days?"

"Well, we usually see him doing something. And there haven't been any lights on. He doesn't go out much. He's usually at home at night."

"Well, thank you very much."

"Is there anything wrong?"

"Not that I know of." Fernandez backed away as quickly as he could and decided to try the house on the other side of Whitney's. There was no answer. He went back to his car. Something was very wrong. He couldn't give himself any reasons, just a cop's intuition.

"QX Four, do you read me?" he said into the car phone.

"QX Four, Captain."

"Put me through to Speke in the D.A.'s office."

A few moments later, Speke answered.

"Can you get me a search warrant right away?" Fernandez said. "I'm at Professor Whitney's house."

"What's happened?"

"I don't know. Just a feeling. He hasn't been seen for several days."

"Christ, you don't . . . I'll get it and bring it down myself."

Fernandez sat in the car waiting. In exactly forty minutes, a patrol car with Speke in it rolled up and stopped. Fernandez got out of his car.

"That was fast," he said to Speke.

"I took a chopper to Valley Division."

"Got the warrant?"

"Right."

They started for the house followed by two patrolmen from the car. One of the officers prized open the rear door and then went in. They found Whitney in the study. He was sitting in a leather armchair with a blank look on his face. One of the patrolmen checked his pulse.

"He's alive. Barely."

"Whitney?" Fernandez said. But the vacant eyes stared past him.

"What's the matter with him?" Speke asked.

"I don't know." Fernandez turned to one of the officers. "Get an ambulance." He turned back toward Whitney. The professor's eyes were deep set, sunken in black shadows, his face drawn. "Whitney?" Fernandez said again. He waved his hand in front of Whitney's eyes but there was no reaction.

"What's the matter with him?" Speke asked again, moving up.

"I think he's catatonic." Fernandez leaned over Whitney, immobile in the chair. "The waxy rigidness."

Speke leaned over too, as if to confirm the diagnosis. He didn't comment. Fernandez started to look around the room. On the desk he found the photostats of the book. The tape recorder had switched off automatically. Fernandez rewound the tape a bit and listened. It was Nelson's tape. The rest of the house seemed to be in order.

The ambulance took Whitney to the hospital and Fernandez followed. He waited for some time until the doctor finally came out.

"Well?"

"I think you're right, Captain. It could be catatonia, brought on by severe shock."

"Shock," Fernandez repeated. The doctor nodded. "Will he come out of it?"

"Can't say."

"What are you going to do with him?"

"I'd like to have him up at Camarillo for observation. They can handle this sort of thing much better."

"I'll get on it," Fernandez said, thinking of the formalities necessary to commit the professor for observation to the State Mental Hospital. "Meanwhile, I want you to keep him under wraps. No one is to see him. I'll arrange a twenty-four-hour guard."

"As you wish."

The doctor went back to his duties after Fernandez completed his instructions. When the police captain got back to the office, he started an investigation on Whitney.

Three days later, he had his answers. Military records, medical checks at the university, the background of Whitney's life showed him to be a strong-minded man with no proclivity toward mental disease, and a most unlikely candidate to suffer catatonia. It didn't add up. Whitney lived a quiet life and was a man of even temper with a reputation for unflappability.

The corridors of Camarillo were not pleasant. It was not so much the look of the place, but a feeling that, but for the grace of God, any of us might be found behind the grim, locked doors. There was an ominous quiet, punctuated from time to time with wild screams, and then silence again. The whole atmosphere of the place made Fernandez' skin crawl. And Dr. Frankel did little to dispel his feelings of disquiet. The doctor was one of those gray people who seemed separated from the world, an observer rather than a participator, with colorless eyes and an expression of perpetual waiting. He let Fernandez look through the peephole. Whitney was sitting in the same way, the same blank look on his face.

"I've had several sessions with him," Frankel said. They were walking back down the corridor to the doctor's office. "I can't tell you much. We've given him shock treatment and drugs. He comes out about halfway, then sinks back again. The withdrawal is deeper each time."

"Do you think he'll ever be normal again?"

"No." It was a clean, flat statement, offering no hope.

"What could have caused it?"

"Shock, probably. Severe shock of some kind. But I can't imagine what it could have been. Based on the psychological reports you supplied us from the army and the university, I'd say there was almost no chance of this man ever suffering a slight neurosis, let alone this. It doesn't add up."

They sat down in the doctor's office. Frankel handed some papers to Fernandez. "These are the transcripts of our last session. You can see the various drugs we tried. But that's all we got. One word: 'Them'. That's all he would say. Then some kind of horror would overcome him and he'd sink right back. His physical reactions were massive: quick heartbeat, rapid pulse, sweating, thrashing."

"Could he have been on drugs of some kind?"

"No." Frankel took the papers back and slipped them in his center drawer. "You know, if I didn't know the facts, I'd say he must have seen something really horrendous. I can't imagine a man like him reacting in such a way to information of any kind. It had to be something really terrible. Some kind of delusion might fit another case history, but not this one. Anyway, whatever it was was so immense, so shattering, that his mind could not cope. And I'd have to say it was an *outside* stimulus in his case. But even so, I couldn't risk a guess."

"You don't think some kind of bad news could have been the cause?"

"It's always possible, but as I say, given Whitney's known personality, it's unlikely. As far as we know, he had no emotional entanglements. His parents are dead. He isn't married. His life was his work. Even," the doctor emphasized by knocking his forefinger on the desk, "even if he had been emotionally involved with someone, I just can't see any news causing this. Let's say he had been married and deeply in love. A man like this would not react to his wife's death in such a way."

"Do you think you can get any more out of him?"

Frankel shook his head slowly. "Whatever it is, he can't face it even under euphoric drugs. And those drugs cut through most things. No, every time we get him out a little, he sinks back even further. I think it would be dangerous to try any more for the time being. He's practically beyond contact now. Still, one never knows. Sometimes they can come out of it for a while . . ." He shrugged.

"There's nothing you can try?"

"We've tried it all. I wouldn't have except that your office seemed to think it was important. Can you give me any idea of what's behind this?"

"I don't know myself."

"Then I have to tell you, in my professional opinion he will never get better, and will probably get worse."

Fernandez went out to Santa Monica pier to buy some lobster. It was a place he often went to when he wanted to think. When he left Camarillo, he drove down along the beach. While his lobsters were being split, a sight he did not relish, he walked out to watch the fishermen and the people on the beach below. Whitney's sickness was another nail in the coffin. Had he told Frankel his own thoughts the doctor might well have kept *him* at the hospital! There was no doubt about one thing. Whoever touched that damned book had something terrible happen to him. Fernandez looked out over the shining Pacific and tried to make sense of it. However much he rejected the conclusion, he could only come back to one point—the book had something to do with the murders.

Ralston was home when Fernandez arrived. It was almost seven o'clock.

"Carol knows all about it."

"All right, let's talk. Am I interrupting dinner?"

"Why don't you stay?"

"I've got a better idea. I've got some fresh lobster in the car. Why don't we have that?"

"Well," Carol said, "you explain it to Annie. She's planned the dinner."

Fernandez smiled grimly and went out to the kitchen. When he came back, he heaved a sigh. "She's a tough customer."

While dinner was being prepared under protest, the three of them went into the study for drinks; Carol brought out some marinated herring she'd been saving. They piled it liberally on rye bread and settled back.

"There's no point in beating around the bush," Fernandez said, munching a bit of herring. "You can guess what this is all about."

"Something new?"

"Yes."

Carol and Ralston exchanged questioning but concerned looks. "Another murder?" Ralston asked.

"No. Whitney's gone mad."

"The professor?" Ralston said, incredulously.

"The same. At this moment he's in Camarillo, a hopeless catatonic."

"What happened to him?"

"Nothing, as far as we know. He had a nice, normal day on Friday and went home. That's the last anyone saw of him. That is, until we found him a few days ago. He was sitting in his armchair, totally withdrawn. As far as we know, he never left his house. He had no emotional involvements, so it's unlikely that a phone call would have thrown him off course so violently. But the crux of the matter is, he simply wasn't the type. Whatever shook him must have been really terrific."

"Is that all?"

Fernandez shifted uncomfortably. "No. And you know it. He was working on your book."

They all sat silently trying to piece together the facts. Finally, Ralston asked, "Are you convinced now the book has something to do with it?"

"Cary, I won't lie to you. I think it's utterly impossible. But I've sifted through every fact and I can come up with only one connecting link—your book. Though I would appreciate your keeping this connection between ourselves."

"You don't have to worry."

"Have you done any more to break the code, Cary?"

"Not directly. I decided I needed some background knowledge first. I've been reading up in math, astronomy, and physics. And I bought a text that Whitney suggested."

"Okay, so what do you know?"

"As far as translating the book, it would be pretty tough, certainly without an expert such as Nelson. As far as the symbols are concerned, I know that Markham thought there was some connection between them and mathematical formulas. I have some of his preliminary notes here."

"You never told me that before," Fernandez admonished, but not severely.

"You didn't put much stock in that sort of speculation."

"All right. You've made your point. Go on."

"Well, that's about it. I sent away to London for some more specialized books on languages—Aramaic, Syrian, Archaic Syrian, Persian, and Egyptian."

"Why those?"

"Because Nelson thought the writing bore some similarity to Middle Eastern languages, though he could not find specific links when he started translating."

"You think the key to all this is in that book. So how do we go about breaking the code?"

"I've been thinking about that. Obviously, it's dangerous the way we've been going. But we don't have any more experts the caliber of Nelson, and even if we did, it might be difficult to enlist their support. They might not be interested in a general project, and if we explained it further, they would probably think we were cranks. Of course, we could tackle it from the math side."

"But you're still skirting the issue," Carol said. They both looked at her. "Maybe you have the wrong experts."

"What kind would you suggest?" Fernandez said, almost dreading the expected answer.

"Someone who knows something about magic, ancient lore, or ESP. There are experts, you know."

"Well . . ." Fernandez started to say.

"She's right, Bob. As a matter of fact, I've already looked into it. The best man for our purposes is a fellow named Hatchett at Harry Warren Thurston University."

"Where the devil is that?"

"It's a small liberal arts college in New Hampshire. I chose him for a number of reasons. First, he's head of the Parapsychology Department there. He's worked with Dr. Rhine at Duke. But he's gone a little farther into the occult. At Duke, from what I understand, they are mostly concerned with ESP and related subjects. This man Hatchett is also something of an archaeologist. But he does deal with supernatural phenomena. He investigates poltergeists and things like that."

"Poltergeists," Fernandez repeated, in a tone that indicated he could hardly believe he was involved in such a conversation.

"Look, this fellow's a professor and well thought of. He's not some crackpot. He's a scientist."

Fernandez considered the idea for some time. "You're getting ahead of me."

"I don't think so. There's a mystery surrounding that book that can't be explained in natural ways. Our only answer is to get someone used to explaining weird happenings. You will be happy to know that he usually explains them in pretty ordinary ways."

"I don't suppose I can afford to leave any stone unturned . . ." the policeman said, to convince himself.

"You can't."

"All right, dammit, I must be out of my mind, but I'll make a deal with you. You set up something with this Professor Hatchett and I'll go with you." They sat in silence until Annie opened the door and angrily told them dinner was served.

"We're coming, Annie," Carol got up. Annie disappeared again.

"Okay." Fernandez said as if finishing some unspoken argument. "Okay."

Harry Warren Thurston University was a quiet little campus, a few colonial buildings around green lawns, with two or three more modern ones scattered behind. The contrast to the hustle and bustle of UCLA was so marked Ralston and Fernandez felt as if they had stepped back into another century. The taxi let them off at the Administration Building and they were directed to one of the new buildings, secluded in a small wood, by a placid lake.

Dr. Corin Hatchett was six feet four with a tousled mop of gray hair. He was open and friendly and almost immediately they felt at ease in his presence. "Gentlemen, please come in." His office was spacious, furnished with antiques, quite a contrast to Whitney's or Nelson's small cubicles. It had a large window overlooking the lake and woods. To both Ralston and Fernandez, it was the sort of place they thought existed only in movies about wealthy professors. The room was lined with books on every wall and there were various bits of sailing bric-a-brac. Hatchett noticed Ralston's interest in an old sextant. "Seventeenth century."

"You have quite a number of them."

"We're an old Yankee family. Most of my ancestors were seamen. Please, sit down."

"You want to begin?" Fernandez said to Ralston.

"Okay, but, Doctor, what we will say is strictly in confidence. Part of the story involves a murder investigation."

Fernandez took out his wallet and showed it to Hatchett.

"I'm a police captain. It's a little out of the ordinary for me to be here . . ."

Hatchett smiled easily, "Most people don't come here about the ordinary, Captain. But set your minds at rest. I certainly will treat all this confidentially. As you can imagine, we often work under such conditions."

Satisfied, Ralston went through the now-familiar story, with Fernandez adding bits of information from time to time. When they finished, Hatchett sat for a long time deep in thought.

"It is a most peculiar story," he finally said. "Most peculiar. Maybe it would be best to first give you an idea of what we do here. Basically, we study parapsychological phenomena. That means things that are outside normal human existence and experience. The bulk of our work centers around the extrasensory abilities of the human mind."

"ESP," Fernandez said.

"Partly. ESP, in layman's terms, means thought transference. Some people have the ability; probably we all do, but we don't know how to use it. We also study clairvoyance. That is the knowledge of things that are happening elsewhere; knowing a loved one is hurt, or seeing a great fire five thousand miles away. There is evidence of that too. People *have* told of events happening many miles away of which they could have had no prior knowledge. So clairvoyance might be called long-distance ESP. Are you with me so far?"

"These things are really possible then." Fernandez seemed to accept it.

"There's no question. To take ESP a step further, we run into precognition, or predicting events that have yet to happen."

"On that point I remain a skeptic," Fernandez said.

"Good. Remain that way. It'll give us a sense of balance as we go on. But let us assume, as Einstein himself stated, that by traveling in the reverse direction of time and space, a man would *physically* be able to go back in time. If the mind has these extrasensory powers, could it not receive impulses along the curve of space? If a mind can travel the distance of several thousand miles instantaneously to see what's happening on the other side of the earth, are there limits to its ability to travel even farther? There is a principle in our work called retrocognition, that is, seeing past events. You get into questions of reincarnation then, but I'm not going that far. I'm speaking of the mind as a sending and receiving set with the apparent ability to move outside the walls of its physical environment. You have to agree, it would be easier to transport thoughts than move the physical body of man."

Fernandez shrugged half-heartedly.

"So if you put together extrasensory perception and Einstein's theories, it *is* possible to conceive of precognition or retrocognition. According to Einstein, you can travel forward or back in time the same way."

"What about telekinesis?" Ralston asked. Fernandez shot him a sharp look.

"I was coming to that. Telekinesis is the apparent ability of some minds to *will* the movement of physical objects. We have very little solid evidence on this. We have not been able to duplicate it in laboratory experiments, but there are cases which tend to show it happens. We also call this ability PK, for 'psychokinesis.' I must tell you that from what we have learned in the last few years, there may be *no limits* to the power of the human mind. Gentlemen, the three of us here today use only ten to fifteen percent of our brains. Think what the other eighty-five or ninety percent might do."

"Are there any reasons why we only use part of our brains?" Ralston said.

"In some cases, it may be what we have forgotten. We certainly had keener sense of smell and hearing in ages past. PK leads us into other areas. Now, if a mind can move a table, can it move something bigger? Well, there are those who say the statues on Easter Island were erected by the concentrated PK effort of a lost race. It could be one of those abilities man had and lost. There are also some who say that alchemists who succeeded in their experiments to change the molecular structure of elements did so the same way. The powers were brought to bear by long and deep concentration."

"In other words, an alchemist could change the chemical composition by PK?" Ralston said, and then looked over to Fernandez, who seemed more skeptical than ever. "Although we haven't demonstrated PK," the professor said, smiling at Fernandez, "we have conclusively proven ESP in our laboratories."

"All right," responded the policeman slowly, "but how does all this apply to our case?"

"I was just giving you a general background. Let's take Professor Nelson's claim to have seen the murder of Ferguesson. It could have been clairvoyance."

"You are not sure?" Ralston asked. "Isn't it the only possible answer?"

"I don't know yet."

"But you do think it was possible for him to have experienced the scene through clairvoyance."

"It *is* possible, Captain."

"I'll have to take your word for it."

"You don't. We'll run a couple of experiments for you. In fact, you can even participate. We might even discover you have talents in the field." Hatchett grinned.

154

Ralston, who had been silent, suddenly said, "Could we go back a bit? When you talk about PK, does the person with the power need to be close to the object?"

"Normally."

"Well, would it be theoretically possible to use that power over a distance?"

Hatchett thought for a moment. "I've never run across it before but, yes, I suppose we'd have to say it was possible. I told you, there are no limits that we know of to the power of the mind." Hatchett paused and looked out the window for a few brief seconds, then turned back to Ralston. "I think I see what you are getting at."

"Would you mind letting me in on this conversation or are you two doing this with ESP?"

"I think Mr. Ralston is wondering whether Professor Nelson could have used a long-distance PK to cause the death of Mr. Ferguesson."

Fernandez stared at them both as if they were crazy. "And you think that that's possible?"

Hatchett shrugged. "Anything is possible."

"I don't know what I am doing here." Fernandez hit his forehead with the heel of his hand.

"Captain, if you'd bear with us just a bit longer. We're just getting into this."

"Okay. Go on," he said glumly.

"Let's leave parapsychology for a moment. You mentioned other matters and perhaps I can throw a little light on the subject. But I warn you, we are getting into fields of sheer speculation. All I can do is describe the myths and try to point out a few scientific possibilities. You mentioned the Necronomicon."

Ralston leaned forward eagerly. "It was in the notes in the back of my book."

"The Necronomicon was a fictional book invented by

H. P. Lovecraft. It was supposed to contain the keys to reach the Ancient Old Ones who lie sleeping in the center of the earth. They were the preterhuman species."

"Come again?" Fernandez said.

"The race that lived on earth before man."

"I see," the captain said cynically.

"Captain, I am only telling you the legend. I didn't say I believed it. Lovecraft actually dreamed all his stories. Now the Ancient Old Ones supposedly had enslaved mankind. Later, they became decadent, died out, and man took over the earth. But, according to Lovecraft's story, they are waiting to come back. The Necronomicon was the means to contact them. In fact, the other books you said were mentioned in the notes were also suggested by Lovecraft."

"So it's all made up?" Fernandez muttered.

"Yes and no. Some people thought Lovecraft's dreams were, in fact, revelations and, therefore, that the Necronomicon *does* exist."

"Do you think that?" asked Fernandez.

"I rather doubt it."

"That's more encouraging."

"You're a hard case, Captain Fernandez." Hatchett laughed, not in the least put off. "What is interesting is that notes naming those books should be found in yours, Mr. Ralston."

"You mean my book *is* one of those?"

"Not necessarily. But surely, whoever wrote those notes thought there was some connection between your book and the mythical ones. I think you're right too, Mr. Ralston. Since Lovecraft died in 1937, the notes were probably written in modern times, most likely by your baron."

"I know I shouldn't be asking this," Fernandez said with

whimsical self-admonition, "but then what is the book Ralston has?"

"It is possible," Hatchett said on reflection, "that it is the Necronomicon, but unlikely. What *is* possible is that it is something *like* the Necronomicon. That could be anything from the general to the specific. It could be a grimoire, that is, a book of magic. And it could be, as Professor Nelson hypothesized, a book of science mistaken for a book of magic."

"In other words, Dr. Hatchett, it could be anything."

"In other words, Captain, it could be. I would have to see it before I could make any stab at that and even then, I might not have any better luck than Nelson."

"Then we have to consider Nelson's theory that the book was the product of some vanished civilization," said Ralston.

"That is right," Hatchett replied. "Cro-Magnon man had a larger cranial capacity than *Homo sapiens*. Was Cro-Magnon man the descendant of a superior race which had fallen back into savagery? Did *Homo sapiens* drive Cro-Magnon away, to a place where he developed his full brain capacity and a super-civilization? It is possible too, that with better living conditions, diets, and so forth, they might have developed greater stature than *Homo sapiens*."

"Giants," Fernandez said.

"In a way. But remember, you and I would be giants to medieval man. 'Giant' is a relative term. To me, a pro football end looks pretty big."

"Okay, but what has all this to do with that book?" Fernandez insisted gently.

"I'm getting to that. Let us assume that there were survivors of an earlier, very sophisticated civilization. Then let us further assume that some of them possessed the infinite scientific knowledge. Being giants, they may have come into a hostile world. Mind you, they might not have been giants—they might have just looked different. So they would group together in a safe place. That place might be Mount Olympus. This is pure supposition, Captain," Hatchett said, before Fernandez could complain. "There they are, a little community, trying to protect themselves from man. Perhaps they did a few tricks, like the first white explorers setting off black powder to frighten the Africans. Perhaps they did mingle with men *and* interbreed. Perhaps, somewhere along the way, their book of science is mistaken for a book of magic. But let me get back to the point. According to what you have told me, these deaths could not have happened through any physical force that we know of. Therefore, I must conclude that your book did indeed have something to do with all this. I think very likely it unlocked powers which none of the victims understood. It is possible that it contains scientific knowledge, which seems quite likely from what you tell me about Professor Markham. And I don't think we can discount the idea, either, that studying the book might have activated latent mental powers."

"You can't really believe that," Fernandez moaned. "It's pure fiction."

"So was space travel a few years ago. I don't see what other conclusions we can come to."

"I agree with him, Bob," said Ralston. "It's what I've been thinking all along. I don't understand it, but I think Dr. Hatchett has put it very logically."

"Logically? You can also argue logically how many angels can stand on the head of a pin. Well, I don't know. Do you really believe in these myths?"

"I don't say that's the answer, Captain. I cite it as a possibility. A book such as that might have been the product of another Einstein who lived many years ago. Surely, you can't say *that* is impossible."

"No," he answered hesitantly. "So what do you suggest?"

"That we get to work on it. I'll come out to Los Angeles."

"If it's what you say it might be," Ralston said, "isn't it likely to be dangerous?"

"Yes. But I'm willing to take the risk." Hatchett leveled his gaze on them both. "If we want to travel to new worlds, we have to take risks, just like an astronaut."

"You know, there's just one thing you seem to be overlooking," Fernandez said. "If no one who read the book understood it, how could they learn anything from it?"

"That's a damned good question, Captain," said the professor. "I can only offer guesses. Markham appeared to have made some progress. We can't be sure how much he did understand. There is the concept of immemorial memory. It is easier to relearn something than learn it for the first time. According to the best authorities, man never forgets anything. All information is stored in his brain. He can't always reach it, but it's there. In the same way, others contend that there is a racial memory. As a matter of fact, it's another explanation of retrocognition."

"You're getting ahead of me again."

"All right, call it instinct. Why do dogs circle around before they sit? To make sure nothing is in the grass. It is instinct from the days when they lived in the wilds. They do it even when lying down on a carpet. How do they know? Instinct . . . and that is another name for immemorial memory. Why does a man turn when someone comes up behind him, even though none of his senses record the presence? Man has instinctual knowledge. Every time we learn something, a groove is made in our brain. If that groove is made time and time again, it becomes an inheritable characteristic."

"Then the book would be a sort of refresher course," Ralston said. "I wonder how much man *could* remember."

"Perhaps everything, Mr. Ralston. Perhaps all. I told you, there are no limits to the human mind."

"What do you want to do, Dr. Hatchett?"

"As I said, I'll come out to Los Angeles. I'll want to round up a few people to help. I'll need some equipment. And I think we ought to keep this quiet."

"You can depend on me," Fernandez said. "I sure as hell don't want anyone to know about it."

"First we look over what we have to do and then we can make further plans."

"Are you sure you want to get involved in this?" Ralston asked.

"Absolutely. This is the only chance I've ever had at a legendary grimoire, Mr. Ralston. I wouldn't miss it for the world. I'm convinced we're going to find out some startling things."

"I hope you're still alive when it's over," Fernandez warned.

"I hope so too. But, this is more my line of country than it was for those other people."

"I don't know," Ralston said. "The Baron de Chantille was mixed up with black magic."

"This has nothing to do with black magic."

"How can you be so sure?" Fernandez questioned. "I thought anything was possible."

"Point well taken. Well, if it is, then I'll worry about that when the time comes. I'm still a scientist, Captain.

Between you and me, I don't believe in the supernatural. But I do believe in the power of the human mind."

"That is the best thing you said all day," Fernandez said. He was genuinely relieved to hear it.

CHAPTER NINE

Meeting Hatchett had accomplished one very important thing; Ralston felt no longer alone. He no longer doubted his own sanity. Someone else, a man respected in the field, believed there was a foundation for all the wild and uncertain guesses he had made. It was true that Hatchett emphasized his own lack of belief that those guesses were true, but he also had an open mind and did not discount the possibility of finding answers that might prove astounding. In a small way, he had been justified. An expert investigator was going to finally set the problems to rest. Hatchett gave no guarantee that he could find a satisfactory explanation, but for Ralston, it was enough that a man of his stature would spend any time at all on the problem.

Fernandez' attitude was quite different. He didn't for a moment accept the possibility of there being an answer couched in such mythical terms, but he could not afford to overlook any chance of a reasonable explanation. If they found one, he would be relieved to hear it. But if they didn't—or if the explanation turned out to be something supernatural—he just did not want to know.

When Ralston arrived back in Los Angeles, he told Carol all that had happened. At first she was displeased that

Cary was even more excited with the study of the book. She had hoped that he would forget about it, turn his mind back to the law and their own lives. But then, with one of those mysterious female quirks, she invited Hatchett to stay with them. Ralston was delighted at the idea. In that way, he could stay on top of the affair even if his law practice occupied his day.

By agreement with Dr. Hatchett, Ralston was not to attempt any further private study of the book. But this did not prevent him from continuing his general readings in physics, math, astronomy, and the art of translating lost languages. At least he would be able to talk intelligently on those subjects and understand what was said to him.

In the meantime, Hatchett made his plans carefully. He would need various pieces of equipment. Ralston agreed to take delivery. The doctor was very pleased to accept Carol's invitation and even more delighted that the garage could be converted into a makeshift laboratory to house his equipment. For one thing, it would lessen the cost and make the university bursar more amenable to other requests. The next order of business was to carefully select his assistants. Doug Scott and Mary Beth Wilson would work with him at Ralston's house; the others could stay at the college. The latter were not to be told the exact nature of the study or who was involved except himself. Hatchett had two reasons for the precaution: first, to prevent his aides from subjection to any long-range powers, such as perhaps had befallen Ferguesson, and second, so they could carry on should anything happen to the prime group. He discounted the idea of any danger being involved, but there *had* been several deaths, so he did not want to take any unnecessary risks. He then made arrangements with several colleagues in the fields of math, astronomy, physics, chemistry, biology, and several other sciences to be available for consultation during their summer holidays. None of them questioned him regarding the project; all knew his field but respected his down-to-earth approach. Finally, he secured permission from UCLA to use Nelson's computer and laboratory. Satisfied that all was in order, he flew to Los Angeles on June 20.

After unpacking, Hatchett came downstairs to have cocktails with Carol on the terrace. It was a beautiful evening and the soft, rich smells of the sea drifted through the garden on a light breeze.

"What a lovely evening," he said. "It's such a pleasure to get away from that sticky heat on the East Coast."

"I ought to warn you. June's our foggy month," she said.

Hatchett ran his fingers through his shock of gray hair. "This is the first time I've been to California." He added, with a twinkle in his eyes, "You don't seem to have many ghosts."

Carol started to smile but then her expression grew serious. "I take it that you're an expert on such things."

"And that worries you."

"As you said, we don't have too many in California."

"Let me put your mind at rest. There don't appear to be many elsewhere either. We've certainly never been able to confirm their existence."

"But you do investigate ghosts . . ."

"Yes," he said equivocally, "but that's not primarily what parapsychology is about. We're mainly interested in studying various phenomena of the mind."

"Then you don't think that book has any . . ." She searched for a word that would not make her seem superstitious or foolish.

"Magic power? No, I don't."

"Cary seems to think the book has something to do with those deaths."

"Perhaps, but not of itself. It may contain knowledge, but that's all. Touching it won't cure warts."

"I'm relieved to hear you say that. Cary has been so wrapped up in all this that sometimes . . ."

"That sometimes you think he's been carried away."

"Well, yes, now that you say it."

"And you'd rather that I hadn't come." Hatchett cocked his head questioningly.

Carol hadn't really wanted to get into the subject, but she said, "To be honest with you, no. I've always felt there are things that ought to be left alone. I don't mean that I'm superstitious, but we don't know all the answers, do we?"

"Not by a long shot."

"At the same time, I feel better having you here. Cary would have gone on with this alone. I'd rather have someone around who knows something about these things. Tell me, when you investigate things like ghosts, do you usually find an answer?"

"If by that you mean a plausible explanation, yes, usually I do. But not always. In my view that is not because there is no explanation, but only that I haven't found it."

"So there could be a plausible answer for what's been happening around that book?"

"I *hope* so."

"I suppose that depends on how we define 'plausible'?"

"You're a clever woman, Mrs. Ralston. Yes, unfortunately there are no absolutes in our world, not anymore. Everything is relative."

"That sounds evasive."

"I don't mean to be."

Carol took some almonds from the dish and nibbled them pensively for a moment. "Doctor," she began, "Cary said you thought telekinesis could have been responsible for Ferguesson's death. I don't really understand how. I don't mean to sound impolite. This is your field. But I just don't understand how something like that could happen."

"I can try and explain it. Try to think of the human mind giving off electrical impulses. We know that it does. That makes it a little more concrete. Telekinesis means the ability of a mind to move or alter physical objects. There are reported cases. Sometimes it is the only rational explanation. For example, you've heard of levitation."

"Only vaguely."

"People who fly, or at least lift themselves off the ground. In the old days, it would have been called witchcraft. If we accept that the power of the mind can lift a table off the ground, there is no reason not to believe that it could also lift the body it's in. We can't put any limits on the power of PK. I believe the human mind does have this ability. I don't know *how* it's done, but I do know it *is* done."

"Even if I accept there is such a thing . . . could telekinesis tear a man into little pieces?"

"Theoretically yes. In any case, I prefer to think in those terms rather than that Ferguesson was killed by some demon raised up by black magic."

The logical progression of Hatchett's argument could not be denied, but Carol still could not quite swallow the concept. "All right, even if I go that far, I don't believe Professor Nelson would do such a thing. I knew him, Doctor. He was a kindly man, like yourself, not a murderer."

"Consciously, probably not. But we are all two people, Mrs. Ralston . . . the conscious and the subconscious. We cannot control our subconscious . . . and, in fact, very often it controls us."

166

"Then you think he could have done it without knowing."

"I only say it's possible, nothing more."

"But how could that book release those powers in Professor Nelson? It couldn't happen just by his looking at it, could it?"

"That is what we have to find out."

"I feel like such a fool for not being able to accept everything you say. You know so much more than I do about these things."

"Please, don't apologize," he said graciously. "There are many people who can't accept parapsychology. The trouble is that so many incidences of it are surrounded by quackery and this has given a bad name to those investigating the phenomena. Once I was called in to look into the practice of a medium. There was no doubt she was a fake *but,* while she was in her so-called trance, the table elevated. I went over that room with five assistants and we couldn't find any mechanical device. There were only two conclusions: I simply hadn't been able to find the device or the medium had PK power to levitate the table. If she used PK, she used it to perpetrate her fraudulent soothsaying. So if she had a genuine ability for PK, it was made suspect by the rest of the humbug. Very often, we come across people who have a talent for ESP and clairvoyancy, but they use it to perpetrate fraudulent fortune-telling. There is reason to believe that Gypsies might have a native ability in those fields, but they are all discredited because they have a reputation for dishonesty and chicanery. I would only give you the advice I give to all my students—keep an open mind. If the facts lead you to a conclusion, don't run away from it, no matter how incredible it may sound at first."

"You present a pretty forceful case, Doctor, but if I

believed you, then I would worry about the danger involved. After all, several men already have died fooling around with that book."

"I wish I could reassure you, but I can't. I am facing an unknown. For myself, I accept the risks just as would a mountain climber or a test pilot. It's my job. But if you mean that there's no reason for your husband to accept these risks, then I would agree with you."

"You don't think he should go on with this?"

"I didn't say that. From my meeting with your husband, I got the impression that he would be hard to stop."

"Have you told me everything? Do I know what all the risks are?"

"Yes, I think you do." Hatchett had wondered whether it was safe to let Ralston remain involved, but Ralston owned the book and if he insisted on being a party to the investigation, there was really nothing Hatchett could do.

"What worries me most of all is that he's an amateur," said Carol. "He's not a scientist and he's not an expert like you."

"There are no experts, Mrs. Ralston," he repeated. "As for being an amateur, your husband has a powerful, logical mind. I'd rather have that than a dozen so-called experts. But if you would like me to have a word with him about dropping the project, I will."

"But it won't do you any good," Ralston said, stepping out onto the terrace. "I want to go on. Doctor, this is the most interesting thing that's happened to me in years. Once, just once, I want to be involved in something constructive, something expansive. This investigation of ours could be my only chance."

After his little speech, Ralston sat down on one of the chaise longues. Hatchett looked over to Carol Ralston. "We might as well settle it," she said, "one way or the other. Cary, I'd rather you didn't go on with this. But if you think it's this important, either to the world or just to you, I'm not going to bitch about it. But I feel you've just rushed into this thing like a kid with a new toy. Do you realize that five or six men have been *killed* fooling around with your book?"

"Yes, sure I realize it."

Hatchett hesitated, unwilling to interfere, but finally his conscience made him say, "If there is any danger involved, Mr. Ralston, it might create a risk to your wife."

That stopped Ralston. He quickly looked over at Carol. The thought had been there, in the back of his mind, but he hadn't been willing to face it. Before he could answer, Carol spoke up emphatically, "That's a bit unfair, Doctor. If it's a question of Cary facing danger, then I want to face it with him." She turned to Ralston, adding, "I'm not trying to sell you. I just wanted certain points made. I've made them."

"Dr. Hatchett's put a different light on it, Carol. I really can't let you take any risks . . . ."

"Cary, if anything happened to you, what would my life be? If something's going to happen, I'd rather it happen to both of us. And besides," she added, "if I were Mrs. Columbus, I wouldn't want it to go down in history that I made him stay home."

Ralston leaned over and kissed her, speaking so that only she could hear. "I love you. You're all right."

He straightened, took a couple of steps looking down at his feet, then said to both of them, "Let me tell you how I feel. I suppose there are people who stay home, don't take chances, and live long lives. But when you think about it, do they live longer than the man who crams in everything he can into life? I don't think so. Better to spend ten years traveling and doing than fifty years watching TV in

169

the front room. We take chances every day . . . we drive, we fly, we ski, or we walk in the park after dark. Some people race cars and some of them get hurt. And for what? For the thrill. Balance that against our taking risks to gain knowledge and I think what we're doing is much more worthwhile."

"Okay, you win. Enough said."

"In all this," Ralston said ruefully, "I forgot to welcome you properly. At least, can I get you a drink?"

"There's a pitcher of Bloody Marys just inside," Carol said.

Ralston popped into the lanai and reappeared quickly with the jug and glasses. "Well, what do we do first?" he asked.

"First," Hatchett said, "I suppose we ought to look at the book. Then we ought to look over Professor Markham's notes. And then we'll have to listen to Professor Nelson's tapes. That could save us some time. After that, we can make our plans. Tomorrow, though, I want to set up my equipment."

"It's all in the garage and the garage has been cleared out. I hope it's satisfactory."

"I'm sure it will be."

"And I've had a telephone installed there as you asked."

"Good. Well then, we seem about ready to begin."

Ralston raised his glass in toast: "Here's to success."

"There *are* a couple of matters I'd like to touch on . . ." Hatchett leaned back in his chair and viewed them gravely. "It's just this. It has to be fully understood that I am in command and I will expect immediate response to my instructions."

"I couldn't agree more," Ralston said rather expansively.

Hatchett folded his hands in his lap. "In my view, Professor Nelson and the others died because they were fooling

170

around with something they didn't understand. There wasn't anyone around who could recognize the signs and call a halt. Well, this time I'm around and when I say stop, we *all* stop. Understood?"

Carol glanced toward Ralston, who answered, "Understood." She felt better.

"Another thing, everything . . . and I *mean* everything . . . that relates to this investigation will be reported to me. I don't care how silly or insignificant it sounds, I want to hear about it. Anything out of the ordinary. Even the wildest idea that pops into your mind."

Ralston nodded his approval. He was impressed by the sharp, crisp authority in the doctor's tone.

"I'll set the work rules." Hatchett continued. "I'll tell you when to start and when to stop. If you feel yourself getting the least bit fatigued, I want to know about it. I'll decide whether you ought to go on. If I order you to rest for a few days, you will. A tired mind is more susceptible. I want all our experiments as controlled as possible. Think of it this way: when the scientists were first working on atomic power, they had a pile with rods which they pulled out little by little. But when the indicator showed the pile was critical, they shoved them back in again without a moment to lose. So when our indicators show that red line, we push the rods back."

"You have my word, I'll follow your instructions faithfully." Ralston spoke sincerely.

"I don't want to give you any false sense of security," Hatchett said. "We all have to be on our toes at all times. You too, Mrs. Ralston."

"Me? What can I do?"

"You can watch your husband for signs of strain, odd behavior, anything that seems peculiar and *tell me about it*. I think that's about it. Oh, yes, two of my assistants will be coming here tomorrow, Mr. Scott and Miss Wilson. If it's all right with you, Mr. Ralston, I'd like Scott to photograph the book with special equipment. He'll have to take it away with him."

"Certainly."

"But he ought to return it tomorrow night. We'll work from the photostats."

"Would you like to look at it before dinner?" Ralston asked.

"Yes, I would."

Carol didn't go down into the cellar with them. Ralston opened the book, which was lying on the worktable. Hatchett peered down at it. "Peculiar script," he said, fingering the writing.

"The symbols are in the second half," Ralston said, carefully turning the pages.

The doctor studied them for a long time. "Paper wasn't introduced into Europe until the tenth or eleventh century, I think. Of course, the Chinese are said to have discovered it in the first century . . . but then, this writing certainly isn't Chinese."

"Then the book must date from when paper came to Europe."

"Uh huh," Hatchett said, still looking at the pages, turning them carefully.

"So that would kind of rule out those lost continents."

"Not necessarily. Of course, the only indication in that direction came from those notes you found."

"Here they are," Ralston said, taking the single sheet from under the cover.

Hatchett studied it for a moment. "We aren't really sure who wrote this." He turned the paper over, then held it up to the light. "There's a watermark. We could check that. It might tell us when and where the paper was manufactured. I'll have Doug Scott run some tests."

"I assumed it was the baron."

"You may be right. In any case, whoever wrote the notes might not have been able to understand the book either. So these could amount to nothing more than doodles or guesses. You said the baron was interested in black magic, didn't you?"

"Yes."

"Well, so that would be the first thing he thought of."

"He might have been able to read the book. The way he died . . ."

Hatchett considered the point. "Yes, it ties in. But then he wasn't any further along than Professor Nelson. He couldn't control what information he'd discovered."

"One thing that has bothered me: if the baron understood the importance of the book, why was it crated up with a lot of pamphlets? That doesn't seem the way you'd treat something you thought valuable."

"You don't know that he put the book in the crate."

"I suppose it could have been the auctioneers."

"From what you told me about the auction, they were in a hurry to sell the stuff off. Perhaps your baron kept the book away from his main library. The auctioneers would only know there was a big book, in a foreign language, not kept with his more valuable collection."

"You mean, they assumed it had no worth. Yes, I suppose that could be. They were rushing, as you said, so if they couldn't find a listing in any of the catalogs, they probably assumed it to be worthless." Ralston thought a moment. "Yes, that makes sense."

"Another thing we do know. This book must have been at the baron's house. Had it been with him in the car, it would have been burned up. So the physical presence of the book means nothing. It's what knowledge it holds . . . *if* it holds any."

"But if this book is only a thousand years old, then it can't have anything to do with the ancient myths."

"Unless it's a copy of an older work. You know, monks used to copy and recopy their precious books when the originals started deteriorating. On the other hand, this could also be an original and, in that case, either it was a recording of something passed along by oral tradition, or what it contains was discovered contemporarily."

"Another Einstein."

"Something like that. Perhaps an Einstein who had some contact with an older cult and worked from what they told him. There are so many possibilities. We can't speculate."

"We can't even be sure the book had anything to do with the deaths."

"Oh, I think we can, Mr. Ralston. Right now, telekinesis is the only possible answer I can think of."

"If you're right, it seems to me that a genius of that period could have discovered how to utilize PK."

"Yes, certainly. He could have discovered it or perhaps he picked up part of it from some cult."

"Why do you keep going back to a cult?"

"Only because of the language. It's fairly complicated, according to what you told me Nelson believed. But I'm not ruling out that our Einstein could have invented it. That kind of power in medieval times would have been treated as witchcraft. A man might have wanted to put it down, but in such a way that only he or his confidants could understand it. Remember, much later than the eleventh century, Galileo said the earth revolved around the sun and got hauled up before the Inquisition. He recanted soon enough. In those days, science ran against the grain of the established religions, in all countries. Well, whatever it is, we have our work cut out for us."

"I don't know how we can approach the problem of language. I mean, neither of us knows much about Nelson's field."

"I'll have some help on that," replied Hatchett.

"You mentioned that before. I was wondering, you say you want to keep this under control, yet you're going to allow these others to work on it. How do you know they won't make the same mistakes as Nelson and the others?"

"Because they will not get the whole picture. I have several people in each field and each of them will see only a fragment."

"Then how can they decipher this?"

"All their findings will filter through me. I will then give them suggestions along various lines. We'll try it this way and that until we get something. It's a bit hit-and-miss, but it's safer."

"Are these people in Los Angeles?"

"I'm afraid that'll have to be my secret. It's another precaution. I hope you'll bear with me."

"I told you, I'll do exactly what you say. Sorry I asked."

Hatchett shrugged it aside. He looked down at the book again. "You know, this could take some time. I don't think it's right for me to stay with you all that time. I wouldn't like to be the man who came to dinner."

"Why don't we cross that bridge when we come to it?"

Hatchett nodded and smiled warmly. "You're very generous."

"Generous, hell. I'm curious. I'd go out of my mind if you were doing this somewhere else. I want to be right on the scene and able to help. By the way, what can I do?"

"For the moment, just be patient. As soon as I get over

the preliminaries, we'll talk and make our plans. I promise I'll keep you informed of exactly what progress, if any, we're making."

For the next few weeks, they discovered little new. Hatchett had the book photocopied with several filters but this brought out no more marginal notes than the one Nelson had found. They even tried several chemical treatments of the original pages, but also without success. Hatchett spent most of his time in the garage, which now looked very much like a small, compact laboratory, working along with Doug Scott and Mary Beth Wilson. The former was a tall, taciturn young man of about thirty; the girl was in her late twenties, studious-looking, with large horn-rimmed glasses. She was not pretty but she adored Dr. Hatchett. Each morning, the doctor left the house early for the garage and did not come back in until dinner time. Sometimes the two assistants stayed for dinner, but more often they ate out and returned to the garage if they intended to work late.

The Ralstons went about their normal business. He went to the office and plodded through the forms and letters that made up his day and she went through her regular routines.

At dinner, Hatchett had little to say about the project. He had studied Markham's original notes, photostats of which Ralston had studied earlier, but the only thing the doctor could glean was that Nelson had had no success—as related on the tape. It was a record of mistakes. Every day great stacks of mail arrived for Hatchett from all over the United States . . . none of them bearing return addresses. And every day Doug Scott would go to the post office around noon to post Hatchett's voluminous replies and queries.

Then one night in July when the Santana was blowing,

Hatchett came to the study after dinner. Ralston was going over briefs and Carol was working on their checkbook.

"I hope I'm not disturbing you," Hatchett said, after knocking lightly on the study door to announce himself.

Ralston sprang up. "Gosh, no. Come on in."

Hatchett came in and took a seat. "I thought you might like to know where we are."

"Are you kidding?" Carol said.

Hatchett grinned. "Well, first I ought to tell you we haven't had any luck with the language."

Ralston sank back in his chair. "It's only been a couple of weeks," he offered, to console himself as much as Hatchett.

"We'll keep at it. But let me tell you what we have found. Remember, I said I was sending out fragments of the symbols to various people. I told each of them what Markham thought of the equation. They all agreed. Markham's theory seems to hold up. The symbols do represent equations. They start with the simplest and work up in difficulty. That's where you can come in. With your knowledge of math, you could work along with us going over what my experts have to say, putting it all together."

Ralston was eager at the prospect. "That's great."

"Now, we've gone along with Markham and in some cases, a little beyond. But the interesting thing is that about a third of the way through the math section, all my experts become baffled. In fact, they all agreed that what they did understand seemed very close to the limits of mathematics."

"What do you mean when you say the math section?"

"Well, since my math people appeared stymied, I got the idea that the symbols might go on into other fields. Remembering that Markham asked for help from a physicist and an astronomer, I did the same. At first, they came up with absolutely nothing. So I studied the symbols further up ahead. I noticed that there are groups of symbols. In other words, we seemed to have a section of symbols which were much the same, then another section, where most of the symbols changed. That went on for a bit and then we got another break in the type of symbols. All right, I took the first few equations of each section and sent them around not only to physicists and astronomers, but also to chemists and biologists. The same thing happened. The chemists and biologists could decipher the equations in their own fields to correspond with simple compounds. Of course, I prompted them. I was using the math experience as a guideline. I should point out that we are nowhere as far along in the other fields as we are in math. Markham did yeoman work."

"Then all those symbols relate to the various sciences."

"It appears so, yes. But let me go back. I told you that my mathematicians were stumped. However, the symbols on the following pages still seemed to relate to mathematics. Assuming that they did, I calculated that my experts had understood about one third of the total."

Carol leaned forward in her chair. "That means you haven't completely solved the code, doesn't it?"

"That's one possibility."

"And the other?" Ralston said.

"The other would be that we understand the code all right, but the information is beyond our present learning."

"I don't know," Ralston said. "There can't be that much more to pure math."

"That's what my experts say. They feel there is very little left to be learned about pure mathematics. Anyway, let me finish. It's what the astronomers have said that's really puzzling. One of them has the idea that one set of symbols represents the sky about five hundred thousand years ago."

"How can he know that?" Carol asked.

"Oh, they can. They compute drifts of stars. They can give you a map of the sky for any date you want."

"But why would there be a sky-chart for five hundred thousand years ago?" Ralston mused.

"That's the question, isn't it? Now, it is possible that some event occurred then which was important. Perhaps it was the date when the planet that ultimately formed the asteroids exploded. One of the chunks could have passed earth causing quite a bit of havoc. That's current astronomical theory."

"Well, that seems reasonable enough," Carol said.

"Unless you wonder how one thousand years ago an astronomer could have known what happened five hundred thousand years ago."

"Right, Mr. Ralston. That might throw us back into our lost civilization theory again. Perhaps the event caused the destruction of that civilization. But five hundred thousand years seems a long time back even for that theory. The supporters of Mu or Atlantis wouldn't go back much more than ten thousand B.C."

"But could the information have been passed along for that long a period?" Ralston asked.

"It would stretch plausibility a little."

"But Dr. Hatchett, if we can compute what the sky looks like today, why couldn't someone have had the same ability a thousand years ago?"

"It's not impossible, Mr. Ralston. However, the scientific aids we have today weren't available then. Still that seemed the most likely explanation until we received this last bit of news. My astronomers are also convinced that there are star-charts which do not reflect *any* known patterns in our sky."

"You said the astronomers weren't sure they were star-charts."

"I did."

"So they must be mistaken." Even though Ralston accepted his own idea at face value, something was bothering him. "But if they aren't wrong . . ."

"Yes?" Hatchett said, asking for expansion of the idea.

"Do you mind letting me in on this?" Carol protested.

"Who could draw star-charts of stars not visible from earth?"

Her mouth dropped slightly. She looked at Ralston, who sat unmoving, then back to Hatchett, whose face was a mask of passive recognition of fact. "You can't be serious" were the only words she could muster.

"Let's not jump to conclusions," Hatchett said. "We don't know that those are really star-charts."

"What do you think the chances are that they are?" she asked, somewhat wide-eyed.

"The astronomer who came up with that idea is one of the most brilliant men in America."

"Does he understand the implication of what he said?" Ralston asked.

"I don't see how he could escape it. An extraterrestrial star-chart is an extraterrestrial star-chart."

"That's fantastic," Carol said.

"You see, we are all forced to the same conclusion."

"I know there's been talk about such things, but really, it's only science fiction." Ralston kept shaking his head.

"I don't know why you find that harder to believe than PK," Hatchett said.

"I can't tell you, except that PK just *feels* more reasonable."

180

"Mr. Ralston, at this very moment there are several large radiotelescopes sending out signals in mathematical binomials to outer space in hopes of contacting intelligent beings. It's being paid for by our government, and several other nations. I don't know of many astronomers today who do not accept the possibility—no, the *probability*—of not only life in outer space, but intelligent life."

"I guess you're right," Ralston said, sagging. "But it just sounds so impossible. You really think they came here five hundred thousand years ago?"

Hatchett shrugged. "Why not?"

"But we can never prove they *are* star-charts.

"True. But if the first lot do prove to be charts of our skies in the past, it adds credibility to the prospect, don't you think?" Hatchett went on quickly before Ralston could answer. "And don't you think there's an interesting parallel here? We send radio messages to outer space in mathematical terms because we believe mathematics has to be understood by intelligent beings. Could the book not be the same? Suppose—just suppose—that whoever wrote that book could not be sure the language would be understood in future years. So he also puts in various scientific equations, formulas and so on. Underneath each one, he explains the same thing in the written language."

"A mathematical Rosetta Stone," Ralston said, catching the idea.

"More than that. A key to unlock the knowledge of the universe."

CHAPTER TEN

◎

Ralston was finding it more and more difficult to bring his mind down from the stars to the everyday problems of corporate forms. The days dragged by; he glanced at the clock continually, waiting until it was a reasonable time for him to leave, then dashed out of the office to race home and go straight to the garage.

But for all the mind-boggling concepts, Hatchett's pace remained unhurried, precise, and detailed. The professor sat at his table, going through mounds of papers and photostats, while his assistants tabulated the results. When Ralston appeared, they accepted that they would leave on various errands—Hatchett wanted them to see only what he wanted them to see.

As soon as Wilson and Scott had gone, Ralston breathlessly asked, "What's new?"

Hatchett pulled his glasses off slowly and rubbed his eyes. "Nothing. A step at a time, a step at a time." This deliberate and unruffled calm made Ralston all the more anxious.

"But . . ." Hatchett went on, looking serious, "I think we're ready to start putting things together. And I want you to understand. You've asked to be part of this and it's your right since you own the book. I think we can be reasonably certain that this book has the ability to trigger latent powers in the human mind. If you join me, things will happen to *your* mind and neither of us can predict what those changes will be. There is a risk. Now I ask you again, are you sure you want to be involved?"

"Absolutely." He offered no other explanation. For a few moments the two men stared fixedly at each other.

"All right." Hatchett put his glasses on with a brisk movement. "The mathematicians have come to a halt. So we can start there. Besides, it's the first section of symbols and one you know something about. As I told you, there have been several men working on the problems. I've given them each a small piece. Taking Professor Markham's ideas, I've made suggestions to help them along. As I said, they seem to agree with Markham's conclusions . . . as far as they went. The only way we are going to see the pattern, if there is one, is by putting the whole together. It's pretty clear you have already absorbed something of it. I refer to your experiences with the guru and the fortune-teller. Therefore, you are susceptible—but you've only been exposed to bits and pieces so far. Now you may be looking at the whole, as far as we can go with it. Two things are very important—one, that you report *anything* to me which seems odd or different, and two, that you *never* work when you are tired. If you've had a busy day at the office, don't come out here. And the very minute you feel even slightly tired, you stop. Understood?"

Ralston nodded. "You'll be working alongside me on the math, then?"

"Some of the time. Sometimes you'll be on your own. I have to keep trying to coordinate work on the other sections."

"How's it coming?"

Hatchett gestured to indicate "so-so." "We've only got a beachhead with chemistry, and a little more with astronomy and physics. Basically, since Markham gave us the key to the math sections, we can make headway with any science that uses math at all. But other fields . . . We'll be lucky to identify them."

"What about the language?"

"Still no luck. The best hope will be when we get a pattern in the math section. Then we'll see."

Ralston felt his stomach fluttering. It was the moment he had both waited for and dreaded. He could be taking the step that might lead him down the same path as the others, or, with Hatchett's better control, that might lead to exciting discoveries.

Initially, Ralston's job was to compare the photostats with the various conclusions of the mathematicians, then compile them, and then look for a repeatable pattern of symbols and translated formulas. These he would then begin to assemble in the order they were in, in the book, by comparing the symbols. It was not as easy as it sounded because some of the symbols had subtle differences, little marks like a circumflex, a tilde, or grave accent. He had to watch carefully, for the addition of one tiny line could make a vast difference in meaning.

When he finally got into it, the very first formula appeared to be nothing more than the numbers 0 through 9. The next set of symbols appeared to be 1 plus 1, 47 minus 90; and those lines were followed in turn by 2 minus 1, 2 times 2, and 2 divided by 2, with varying degrees of complexity illustrating the same point. It was an exciting discovery.

"Like a lesson," Hatchett muttered as they scanned the page.

184

"It's laid out just like a textbook."

"That may be just what it is." Hatchett smiled.

Every evening, Ralston went a little further into mathematical principles and when he had completed only two and a half pages of the book, he was already into algebra. At that point everything still seemed to prove out; the progression from the simplest to the more complicated was true. This time, though, he was seeing the logic of it, whereas before there had been only bits and pieces, mainly because Markham's translation was incorrect in several places.

But the "moonlighting" was taking its effect. Both Carol and Hatchett commented on Ralston's apparent fatigue and enforced two nights of rest, while Hatchett pressed on. That made Ralston even more agitated. He kept going to the window, looking out toward the garage, and wondering what was happening. His curiosity and the feeling of being left out, even temporarily, gnawed at him and pushed him to a decision that had been in the back of his mind.

"Six months?" Reikert said with surprise. The senior partner was obviously disturbed by the request. "That'll throw us into turmoil."

"Not the way I have it worked out."

"But six months. Christ, Cary, if you wanted another month, even two, it's one thing. But you're talking about half a year!"

"Dick, I've been with the firm for six years. Until last spring, I never took a vacation, not even a week at Christmas. You know that. I'm going stale," he said, to give a reason. "I have to have some time away and if you figure a month every year, it comes to six months. I think that's fair."

"A month at a time, sure. Look, Cary, I've got a law practice to run. You can't just dust off your clients like that."

"I don't intend to. If you need me for anything, I'll be available. I can be down here at an hour's notice. And I'll oversee the work that's being done on my cases. Short can knock out the drafts and send them along to me, if there are any client problems.

The older lawyer drummed the table in irritation. "This is rather short notice."

"It's a good time. I haven't got anything pressing at the moment."

"I must say, I would have expected more from you, Cary. I'm disappointed."

Ralston felt himself go hot under the collar, but he kept his voice even. "The thing is, I need a rest. And I'm not going to be any good to myself or to you unless I get it. If what I propose isn't acceptable, then I suggest you and the others can buy out my interest."

"Take it easy," Reikert said hurriedly. The concern on his face was apparent. Not only could they lose Ralston, but he might end up at some rival firm, taking clients with him. "I'll have to put it to the others. After all, as a partner, you still share in the profits, even if you're not working. I don't know how that will set with everyone."

"I'm sorry if I've put you in a tight spot, Dick. But I've made up my mind."

"Rather sudden, isn't it?"

"A bit."

"Has anyone else made you an offer?"

"Nothing like that."

"Are you unhappy with the arrangements here?"

"Not that either. I'm perfectly content with the way things are. I'm not trying to sandbag you."

The older lawyer settled back into his chair with an air of resignation. He knew Ralston well enough to know he would not change his mind. "You honestly think Short can handle most of this?"

"He was top man at Harvard. He probably knows more law than I do."

"You're not planning to go away?"

"I'll be at home."

"Well, I can't pretend I quite understand this. Are you just planning to sit around the house for six months?"

"Something like that."

After Ralston left, the senior partner sat in confusion. He really could not understand why Ralston would have done such a thing. He must have known the strain it would put the whole firm under with their top corporation expert gone. Still, if he was willing to remain on tap and oversee what Short did, there was no reason it couldn't work, and if something really ticklish came up, they could call him in. Ralston would be hard to replace and, if he went somewhere else, it would be worse. There really was no choice. Either they gave him his requested leave of absence or they lost him completely. The other partners agreed to the conditions even though there was some grumbling. And so Ralston won his chance to devote himself fully to working along with Dr. Hatchett.

Carol was a little surprised when he told her. At first she was highly disturbed at his throwing away a brilliant career over a crazy obsession with a myth. "Darling, we've been carried away with this craziness. I've thought a lot about what Dr. Hatchett said the other night. What really astounds me is that you and I were standing there and agreeing it was possible. Cary, it can't be."

"Yes, I have thought about it," he said, trying to console her. "I know it all sounds fantastic but so was the atomic bomb. Hatchett is way ahead of me too, Carol. He's had experience with these matters. Crazy as it may sound, a lot of it makes sense. And I've got to see it through. It's the most fascinating thing I've ever done and the law practice is not going to suffer. I'm still a partner. I get my financial share. And after I go back, all the ruffled feathers will be smoothed down."

Carol sat down heavily, almost on the verge of tears. Ralston came up beside her, took her hand. "Cary," she said, "you know I just started thinking about all this. We've accepted these crazy theories as if they were explanations of how to play Monopoly. It's all so unreal. But we talk about it in an everyday fashion, about lost civilizations, and people from the stars. I wonder if we haven't lost our minds?"

"Sweetheart, it sounds as wild to me as it does to you, but if we don't look for the answer, we're never going to prove any of it."

"What if you find something you don't want to find?"

"Darling, you can't have it both ways. Either this is all foolishness or it's something real to worry about."

"Oh, I'm so damned mixed up, I don't know what I think. I just wish we'd never got involved. I've got a bad feeling about the whole thing."

He sat down on the ottoman and pulled her to him, cradling her gently. "Now don't jump from one extreme to the other. Or have you suddenly gone psychic?"

She brushed away a tear and managed a half-smile. "I guess I'm being silly."

"For a practical girl like you, yes."

"I'm sorry. But Cary, are you sure things will be all right at the office?"

"Absolutely."

"Well, okay." It wasn't for that reason that she conceded; it was an excuse she hung it on. Her problem was simply that while her mind could accept any possibility, her heart could not. Down deep she couldn't really quite believe. "I wonder if it's worth it," she added.

"We won't know until we have the answers. Maybe not. But after all that's happened, I can't believe that either."

"And look what's happened." He felt her shudder when she spoke.

"Darling, knowledge isn't dangerous unless it's misused or half-understood. The only safety is to know *all* there is. Full knowledge is control."

"You believe that?"

" 'A *little* knowledge is a dangerous thing.' Not complete knowledge."

They sat together for some time, he talking soothingly, and Carol softened, until she seemed reasonably assured.

While he cleaned up details at the office, which took him until the end of the week, Dr. Hatchett flew back East. Although Ralston waited anxiously for the professor's return, he enjoyed his absence. He and Carol went out every night—to the theater, the Music Center, and the movies; by Monday, Carol was quite relaxed, her old self, and he was ready to start work full time on the book.

The doctor had evidently arrived late Sunday night and let himself in with the key Ralston had supplied him, for he was hard at work the next morning when Ralston went out to the garage.

"Was your trip a success?"

Hatchett half-shook his head. "Yes and no. We have some more parts to interlace with the others . . . guesses, good guesses. But, we will have to keep plugging at it. The language analysts won't be able to do anything until we can give them a section to compare with the symbols."

"Did you discuss any of your theories with them?"

"No. It's premature. Science is full of skeptics, as it rightly should be. You've got to give them firm evidence."

Ralston sat down at his table and began sorting through the new material. Each mathematician had taken the set of symbols and written opposite what he thought was the formula that it represented. Hatchett had given them variations; some of them had supplied their own. It was Ralston's job to correlate them and choose the ones which coordinated with the rest. Sometimes he put one formula in and later found that it would not match up to subsequent material; often that meant starting again from the same point, until the whole progression flowed one from the other. Then and only then was a pattern barely discernible. Finally, after several days, he ran across a set of symbols which apparently none of the mathematicians had been able to translate.

"That's funny," he muttered aloud. "That should be $MD_3 \frac{Y(2x)}{P-M}$." He looked up to see Hatchett staring at him fixedly.

"What did you say?"

He repeated the equation. "No one seems to have put that down."

"And *you* did?"

"It just seemed obvious."

Hatchett came over and stared down at the equation Ralston had written. "What does it mean?"

Ralston looked at him blankly. "Well, to tell you the truth, I'm not really sure. I know that sounds ridiculous. How could I know what the symbols mean if I don't understand it?"

"Now think carefully. When you were at UCLA, did you study this?"

Ralston looked at the paper again. "I don't think so."

"Could it be something from way back in your memory?"

Ralston shook his head. Hatchett took the paper and went to the telephone. He dialed. "Hatchett here. I wonder if you could tell me what this means." Hatchett repeated the formula as Ralston had written it. "I see. Yes, you can call me back here. KL5–2332." He put down the telephone slowly. "He didn't know it. And he's one of the best."

"Well, I didn't guarantee it," Ralston laughed. "I really didn't expect it to be anything, did you?"

"It was worth a try. But I wonder what made you write it down?"

"I don't know. I tell you, it just seemed obvious."

The two men returned to their labors. Within an hour the telephone rang. Hatchett snapped up the receiver and listened intently. Whatever was said left him profoundly impressed. He was grinning when he put the receiver down. "That man's in the missile program. One of the best mathematicians in the country. He's run your equation through their computer. It appears to be a formula related to a more complete fuel consumption through nuclear fusion." Hatchett read the last few words. He looked up from the paper on which he had hastily scribbled the note. "It's along the lines of something they are working on, but haven't quite perfected. It's also Top Secret."

"But how could I know that? It's way beyond anything I've ever studied."

"Cary, I think you fail to realize. It's way beyond anything *anybody* has studied."

There was an awesome silence as the two men contemplated each other from across the tables and a deep atmosphere of wonderment settled over them.

"How is that possible?" Ralston said at length.

"The book is teaching you. I don't know how, yet. Perhaps it is the sequence or arrangement, I just don't know. But you *are* learning."

"But Professor, I didn't know what the equation meant. I still don't, even after you told me. It just sort of popped into my head. But I don't understand it."

"In time. In time, perhaps you will."

"I can't understand how reading a book I don't understand about subjects I don't understand can teach me anything." There was a desperation in his voice, a frustration at not being able to comprehend something that was apparently happening to *him*.

Hatchett started pacing about, scratching his head and stroking his chin. He moved with a sense of urgency. Then he spun back toward Ralston. "Do you remember I mentioned immemorial memory?"

"Something. The human race never forgets. All our racial knowledge is locked up in our subconscious. Now, wait. How could my racial memory remember things that haven't even been discovered yet?"

"We don't know that. We only know that mankind *today* has not discovered it."

"I can't accept it. I know what you're getting at."

"You see, you could accept the theory, but not now that it's happening to you. *Your* immemorial memory has been triggered. The brain never forgets. It's a computer with all our knowledge stored in it. We have to find the right program to get the information out, to get the information into the conscious. Somehow this book is doing just that, programming, and the input will produce the output. How it happens, I don't know. But we're on the right track. You can't doubt now. The conclusions are inescapable," Hatchett said buoyantly. "Even more important, don't you see, you've got it together the right way. I have to go over it with you now. We have to go over what we have so far until we *do* understand, both of us. Is it all being planted," he whispered with a faraway look, "—all our theories and wild speculations? Are those your ideas or are they being remembered?"

In a way, it was like working on a jigsaw puzzle—one corner had begun to take form. All the gaps were not filled in but a vague outline could be glimpsed. And when that corner was complete, they might have the key to the language of the book. Both men concentrated on the parts of the mathematics section which had been put together. They went over it time and time again and though there were no dramatic breakthroughs, each time it seemed to be a tiny, fractional part clearer.

It was a bright, sunny afternoon and the light was slanting down through the transom windows. A rich smell of newly turned soil filled the garage. The gardener had been preparing new beds for pansies around the sides. Ralston leaned back and stretched, glancing over toward Hatchett, who was deep in concentration. The lawyer much admired the scientist's ability to shut out the surrounding world and pore over his work. A shaft of sun gleamed off Hatchett's gray head and splayed out down onto the pile of photostats and papers on the table in front of him. The light glistened on something shiny and black moving on the doctor's collar. Ralston froze with horror. Pinned in the brightness was a very large black widow spider. Ralston didn't know what to do. If he warned Hatchett, the normal reaction to brush the insect away might cause it to bite; yet to give no warning would probably result in the same thing. There wasn't time to get up, cross to Hatchett, and scoop it aside. Somehow the spider had to be removed; the bite of one so large in such a vulnerable spot could cause death. Ralston could feel the sweat on his brow as he stared with intensity. And then suddenly, the black widow whirled off Hatchett's collar and dashed itself against the wall of the garage. It fell just to the right of a two-by-four that was leaning against the wall. Inexplicably, the bit of lumber tumbled over and squashed the insect. Ralston stared at the piece of wood in open-mouthed amazement.

"Thank God," he exhaled with relief.

Hatchett looked up. "Hmmm?"

Ralston got up and walked over to the piece of wood. He turned it over with his foot. The black widow was squashed on the downward side.

"What is it?"

"A black widow."

"They're bigger than I thought." Hatchett leaned over to get a closer look.

"It's a big one. It was on your collar."

Involuntarily, Hatchett's hand flew up to his collar; then his eyes measured the distance from where he was sitting to the squashed insect. "How did it get over here?"

"I was sitting there thinking of what to do when it suddenly just flew off your collar and hit the wall. If I'd told you, you would have moved your hand just like you did now. It would have bitten you. That happened to a friend of mine. It made him very sick."

Hatchett looked back down at the spider. "And that bit of lumber just fell over?"

"Yes." He glanced up into the older man's face. "Funny, I was hoping it would and then it did."

Hatchett took Ralston by the arm and led him to a chair. "Sit down a minute. I want to know what you were thinking when you saw that spider on my collar."

"I was thinking of a way to get it off."

"And when it flew against the wall . . ."

"I wanted to kill it with the board," Ralston said without thinking, then realized what he'd said. He looked up into Hatchett's eyes. They had narrowed with revelation.

"You *did* it. You moved it off my collar and squashed it with that board."

"PK." Ralston intoned the words. "Telekinesis."

"Yes."

"But I felt nothing . . . I . . ." He shrugged helplessly.

"But you *did* do it. It could have happened no other way." Hatchett took his hand from Ralston's shoulder and stepped back. "It's part of the pattern. Not only memory is jogged, but latent powers."

The lawyer shook his head. "You say it . . . and it makes a certain kind of logic . . . But I wasn't conscious of doing these things. I don't know why that formula popped into my head, but it did. And now this."

"We have to work at it now, bring it under control." Hatchett stepped to the desk and put a pencil down near the edge. "Cary, I want you to move this pencil. Now concentrate."

Half-believing, Ralston looked from the professor to the pencil and back to the professor. Hatchett's face was deadly earnest. Ralston focused on the pencil and concentrated with all his might but the pencil did not move. "It's no good."

"Keep trying!"

Again Ralston forced his mind on making the pencil move, but still nothing happened. At last, he sagged. "No use."

"Then we'll try again tomorrow, when you've rested, and every day until you can do it. And I will too."

"I don't know. This frightens me."

"Why?" Hatchett implored.

"You said there were no limits to PK once."

"That's right."

"And you said PK might explain how Nelson and all those others died."

"Now wait, before you go on. I also think you have a far different temperament than Professor Nelson. Believe me, I didn't come into this without checking. Once you were determined to become involved, I had to be certain I could trust you . . . I mean subconsciously. Believe me, Cary, I would have looked a long time to find a more compatible partner. You are emotionally suitable. You've got a logical mind, a knowledge of mathematics, *and* an even, good-natured temperament."

"You checked on me?" he said with a bemused smile.

"I think you'd prefer me to be thorough."

"Sometimes you amaze me."

"If you had a temper like Professor Nelson, then I could not risk opening these doors."

"It's my subconscious I'm worried about. No one knows what's lurking there."

"No. But there's bound to be some risk," Hatchett said with a smile.

"You seem to be taking this all very lightly."

"I'm enthused. We're making great progress. I told you before, our safety valve is knowledge and the ability to control it consciously. That's why you must learn to do this. Now, what do you say?"

After a moment's pause, Ralston nodded.

"Good, then tomorrow morning."

For the next three mornings both men concentrated on the pencil and nothing happened. Ralston was beginning to wonder if a sudden breeze could not have lifted the spider from Hatchett's collar and blown the board over.

But he rememberd no wind, nor the slightest indication of one. Nonetheless, the lack of result in the experiment disillusioned him and made him doubt.

On Friday night he and Carol decided to eat out, since Hatchett had some research to do at UCLA. They thought they would try a new, small French restaurant on South Beverly Drive that had been highly recommended. It turned out to be a tiny place with tables crowded together so closely that the waiters had to dart skillfully sideways to pass between them. Even that slight inconvenience could not spoil the evening. The restaurant was a perfect re-creation of a St.-Germain cafe, the food was excellent, and Carol looked stunning in her new dress.

"Did I ever tell you I love you?"

"I think you mentioned it once or twice."

"Did I ever tell you you turn me on?"

"Now, calm down, Cary," she said, "we *do* want to come back to this restaurant again."

They found each other's hands across the table. "I do love you."

"And I love you." She turned away, biting her lip for an instant.

"What's the matter?"

She turned back. "I love you and I can't give you a child."

"Honey, you're all I want."

"You're sweet, but you don't mean that."

"Yes I do. We've been through all this."

"I know but . . ."

"But nothing. Just remember we're doing something about overpopulation." He squeezed her hand.

At that precise moment, two waiters tried to pass their table at the same time and one of them brushed against it. It tilted just enough to send the wine bottle reeling toward

Carol. Her hands flew up in panic for it was clear the bottle would fall into her lap and then, miraculously, it righted itself with only a few drops spilled on the tablecloth. Carol stared in amazement.

"That's impossible," she said. Then she stared at her husband. "Cary?"

"Yes, Darling. It was me."

"You?"

"I can do it . . . sometimes . . . in an emergency."

"You made that bottle stand up again?"

He told her about the black widow.

"Why didn't you mention it before? You promised to tell me everything you were doing out there."

"Because I wasn't sure."

"You are now?"

"You saw, Carol. That bottle was falling into your lap. And nothing could have stopped it except . . . PK."

"It's a little scary."

"No. No," he repeated with an idea forming. "It was conscious. It was a conscious attempt to prevent that bottle from ruining your dress. Not something subconscious."

"I wish I knew what the hell you were talking about."

His elation was growing. "It was a conscious effort and that means my control is growing. Hatchett is right."

"Well, that explains it all."

"I'll explain it on the way home. Come on, let's pay the bill."

"Well, there goes a perfect evening."

Hatchett was back in his room when they got home. Ralston eagerly explained what had happened, and it was evident from Hatchett's excitement that he agreed with Ralston. "You're right. And if we can control this thing, consciously, we are well ahead of the others. I feel very good about this. Very good."

198

"But are you any safer?" Carol asked.

"Yes, Mrs. Ralston, we are. We know what to guard against and we are learning how to control it. Nelson and all the others had no idea what was happening to them. No, there's a big difference. Yes, I feel very good about the way things are going."

But their confidence was ill-advised for that same evening they were all to go through the most terrifying experience of their lives.

CHAPTER ELEVEN

◎

Excitement gave way to exhaustion as Ralston crawled into bed next to Carol. She moved close and he put his arm around her. She was asleep in a few moments, but his exhilaration had buoyed him up and his mind buzzed with contemplation of their future work. Finally, though, he drifted off into a deep sleep. His dream was both confused and disorienting, but even so, he experienced a feeling of wonderful euphoria. He seemed to float up away from himself and then soar away from the earth, past the planets, and into the inky vastness of space, rushing headlong amongst the stars but without a sensation of speed. On and on, and faster and faster, he went; power and a sense of command surging through him. He felt another presence, somewhere behind him. He passed through tunnels of light and blackness into a deeper black and light; he coasted through velvety oceans of eternity, down a kaleidoscopic corridor of fiery colors and out again through the voids of space and time, all the while knowing that he was getting closer to something marvelous.

He was standing in a distorted jungle of Picasso shapes and images, vibrant with colors, moving in slow motion with floating steps, like an astronaut on the moon. On he pressed through treelike plants of purples, greens, reds, and all the time he knew that he had a companion though he did not turn to see who it might be. It was like swimming in a warm bath and he was overcome by a feeling of utter luxury and well-being.

It stopped. The good feeling fled with the brightness and light. It was a dark world of bubbling gray mud and potholes, the ground rumbling and pitching under him, a nauseating odor sweeping over him until he reeled. The earth crunched with the oncoming footsteps. He tried to turn. Something shadowy and frightening oozed up out of the slime in the distance, then another. His feet would not move. Try as he would to run, he could only float aimlessly while whatever it was came after him. The viscous, liverish fluid sucked at him, as bubbles popped to emit noxious steams. He pushed back with his mind.

The great black voids flashed by, the tunnels of light and color, the voids of space, but though he was going back, it was coming after him. He could feel its presence closing on him. Terror accelerated his return to himself and then he was awake, bathed in sweat, staring through the darkness of the bedroom toward the door. The stench of that awful place was still in his nostrils. He shook his head, but the flapping of giant wings from the doorway sharpened his senses in an instant. Every nerve and fiber trembled as he strained his eyes against the darkness trying to discover what evil lurked there.

"What's that smell?" Carol said, pushing herself up on one elbow.

Her very words struck Ralston with stark terror. This was no figment of his imagination. She could smell it too. Whatever it was, it was there, there in the room with them!

He concentrated all of his energy against it and then, whatever it was, it moved from the doorway. It was gone—as if it had never been there. He leaned back against the pillows with relief.

"Cary? What *is* that awful smell?"

Her words jarred his senses and shocked him. He knew he ought to say something, but there was no time. He threw off the bedcovers and dashed toward the hallway.

"Cary!"

He ran down the hallway to Hatchett's room and flung open the door. The sight which greeted his eyes filled him with loathing and horror of such magnitude that his whole body wrenched with shock. It was there, hovering over the bed, a monstrous and horrifying thing of consummate evil. Hatchett, wide-eyed with fear, was pressed up against the headboard of his bed. Ralston strained his mind against the thing. And it was gone.

Ralston fell back against the wall, spent. It took him some time to recover his strength, by which time Carol, tying up her robe, came to the doorway and looked in. Hatchett was still sitting up against the headboard, a look of total disbelief frozen on his features. She needed no explanation that something was very wrong.

"Cary?" she said quietly, inquiringly.

"We had a bad dream," he breathed heavily, catching his breath.

"Y-yes," Hatchett murmured. "Would you mind, I think I'd like to have a drink."

"Help yourself. I'll be down in a minute." He put his arms around Carol and led her back to the bedroom.

"Darling, come to bed."

"As soon as I see how Hatchett is feeling."

"He can take care of himself," she said, crawling unwillingly back into bed.

"You go back to sleep."

"All right." He stopped in the doorway and turned back.

"What *was* that smell?" she said.

"Nothing. Garbage."

Ralston tiptoed downstairs. He found Hatchett in the study. Ralston shut the door.

"You saw it?" Hatchett asked.

"Yes."

"A giant, leathery gargoyle," Hatchett said with a tremor in his voice. Ralston nodded. "Those horrid eyes and the tridactyl claws and that beak." Hatchett poured himself another drink and gulped it down. Then he sat down in the armchair and rubbed his eyes wearily.

"What was it?" Ralston decided he could use a drink too. His face was drained and he felt weak.

"I don't know yet. Did you dream?"

"Yes." Ralston told him the dream.

"Yes, that was it."

"You know?"

"I was with you."

"I felt someone was there . . ." Ralston swallowed his drink.

"I was . . . I was behind you."

"Was it a dream?"

"It could have been."

"We had the same one?"

"ESP could operate while we were both asleep. Or it could have been astral projection, an out-of-body experience. Our Ka traveled to that distant place."

"What do you mean by 'Ka'?" asked Ralston.

"It's a term we use to describe what leaves our body. You could call it our spirit or soul. It comes from ancient Egyptian mythology. They thought of the Ka as the double of the corporeal body."

"Then you mean this Ka actually left our bodies and went somewhere . . . through space?" Ralston shook his head incredulously. "It's impossible."

"But you saw the thing." Hatchett thought for a long time. "If it was a dream, suppose we created that thing with our minds, some combination of ESP, a dream, and astral projection. Look, people have described seeing a person, a solid entity, in a place miles from where they actually were. We've recorded those incidents. It would mean that the person was able to reconstruct another image of himself. If that could happen, couldn't two minds reconstruct a dream object? Are you familiar with the holographic film process?"

"No."

"They can project what appears to be a three-dimensional figure, using three cameras focused on a point of space."

"That doesn't explain the smell."

"Any of our senses could have been affected."

"Carol smelled it too."

Hatchett seemed to jolt in his chair. "You're certain?"

"Yes."

"It was there?"

There was another long silence while the two men contemplated what had occurred and the possible implications. Neither could quite cope with the astounding visitation. Yet it had happened and there had to be some explanation. If the limits of their credulity had been reached, the limits of their imaginations had not.

"Cary," Hatchett began tentatively, searching for words, "Something is ticking around in my mind. I'm thinking out loud, but . . . Well, we now know that the book triggers off lost memories and forgotten powers. What we haven't considered are what other powers may have been lost to mankind over the years. All through history, for example, we've had reports of various kinds of psychic phenomena. They've been explained in various ways. It's happened sporadically, an individual here, an individual there. But suppose *all* those powers are latent within each of us, the whole gamut. In other words, the book might be rekindling the whole package in us, even to calling up the Devil . . ."

"The Devil? No, I can't accept that, Doctor. The supernatural I won't buy."

"When I say the Devil, I mean what we saw tonight. Something that was *taken* to be the Devil. Now listen. The powers of astral projection have also been developed in us. Wherever it was that we went tonight, that thing followed us back on the same beam, so to speak, and it stayed only as long as we allowed it. We sent it away . . . or you did. I was too frightened to concentrate."

"PK again?"

"Well, some combination of PK and astral projection— the reverse of astral projection. Look, I'm only groping, but there's an idea buzzing around in my brain." He spoke with growing animation, "All psychic phenomena may be explicable in terms of understanding the contents of that book."

It was a sweeping conclusion of such magnitude that it tested the mind, yet both men could accept it more readily than any supernatural explanation. That all the half-understood and feared manifestations of mankind could be fitted into one pattern seemed a more rational approach than any other yet put forward. No matter how fantastic would be the ultimate answer, the fact that it was one common cause to so many inexplicable happenings made it more reasonable. Both men had been brought up in a world of vast changes. They had lived through several extraordinary experiences in the past weeks. They were ready to explore the darkest corners of human imagination without shrinking.

"All right," Ralston said, "then the first question is where did man get these abilities and why has he lost them?"

"Let's start with where," Hatchett replied. "My guess is, it is where we were tonight, or just beyond. When we were traveling, I had the feeling that I was going to encounter something so wonderful and marvelous . . ."

"Yes, I too, in the beginning. In fact," Ralston said after a moment's thought, "it was almost like going home in a sense. I know that sounds mad."

"It also describes my feelings. It could be that we were returning to the primordial springs, to the atavistic beginnings of our kind."

"If that beast was our ancestor, I'd rather not know."

"I don't think so. No, I think there was something else, something beyond where that beast intercepted us."

"Why did it intercept us? Why did it return with us?"

"To prevent us from reaching Them, whoever or whatever they are. You have to conclude that the beast and They are enemies."

"You mean that with all their power and knowledge they cannot destroy such a loathsome thing as that? It doesn't seem to follow."

"Let's leave that for the moment. I haven't got all the answers. But I can tell you one thing . . . that beast may have been what caused the deaths of Nelson and the others."

"I've already thought of that. But even so, I don't see how they were pulled apart as they were."

"If you think of the creature as antimatter," Hatchett suggested, "if it comes together with matter both would disintegrate. Since it is created by the mind, the mind and the surrounding head disintegrate. But that would not apply to Nelson, Ferguesson, and the others being pulled apart. That's how Nelson used the power. Subconsciously, he wanted Ferguesson torn limb from limb and we know he was jealous of Markham's success with the symbols. Nelson's subconscious called the power into being but it turned back on him."

"That's a neat explanation, as far as it goes." Ralston continued, "But suppose we really didn't *go* anywhere. Suppose we merely had a mutual dream, a remembrance of something from primordial time, something we shared because of ESP? If the book can help us remember lost arts, there's no reason why it might not make us remember the dawn of time—or even recognize our own id, the beast in man. Perhaps that beast was only a manifestation of that, the beast in ourselves. Going back to your idea of the holographic film process, suppose our imaginations created that thing and gave it substance through some aberration of PK?"

"That's a very interesting point, Cary. The id, our primitive nature. But man has two sides, one, the beast and the other, his rational side. Dr. Jekyll and Mr. Hyde." Hatchett stroked his chin thoughtfully before continuing, "Ah, you're proving an apt pupil. You missed your calling. You should have been a psychic investigator all along. Yes, you could explain it that way . . . but then, who wrote the book? That's why I can't accept your explanation. I think that book is not only a mere repository of knowledge, but a bridge, a key, that could unlock even more unfathomable secrets of the universe than it holds itself.

And I think those answers are to be found at the destination we did not reach tonight. Beyond where we were intercepted is what we are looking for."

"If it's like what we already found, perhaps it's just as well to leave it," Ralston responded.

"No, it has to be something better, something truly magnificent. And there's a reason we must go on."

"If this 'They' of yours have such infinite powers, why don't They come to us?"

"I don't know."

"You are completely disregarding the idea of some race right here on earth that was superior to man?"

"Yes. For such a race to develop, it would have taken millons of years before man even appeared on this planet. All geological evidence would deny that. It's more incredible to me that this should have happened than that the seeds of man were grown on some distant world and transplanted. Super races don't erupt like popcorn. It takes time. But when that seed was planted here, it could have developed on one of those Lost Continents and then somehow, through decadence or some other reason, the colony declined or destroyed itself. If we are the image of Them, which I think we must be, then we have their failings as well as their superiority . . . and conversely. If they corrupted themselves, it could be because they were too much like man."

"Even if They have the powers you suggest, They don't seem to be able to control those things," Ralston countered.

"We don't know that. If there are other beings in the universe, even enemies, They may not *choose* to destroy them, merely to keep them at bay. If They do not help us, it may be because we must find our own way to Them."

"You make it sound like this was some sort of test."

"Not in so many words. I didn't mean to."

"How are you and I going to control those things when we have not even learned a fraction of what that book contains? If we fail, we could bring havoc back to earth with us."

"No, I don't think so. As I said, I think these things have made appearances on earth before, but they have always returned to where they come from. In any case, I have to go on because I know that if we reach our goal it will be of immeasurable benefit to mankind. I feel that in my bones. I know it as surely as I can see you standing there."

"Yes, but, we can only do this when we sleep. It's not in control. If we fall asleep again . . ."

"I know, I've thought about that. We have to find some sort of safety device. If we must be asleep to perform this, then the best safety valve would be wakefulness."

"Well, we can't stay awake forever."

"No, but we can be *awakened*. And then, only when necessary."

"How are we going to do that?"

"I've got an idea. Leave it to me. It'll be taken care of by tonight."

"Okay." Ralston had another thought. "What happens if we wake up and our Ka is a million miles away?"

"Once the conditions under which it travels are broken, it will return to the body. The Ka can travel instantaneously because there are no barriers like the speed of light. Once that state of subconsciousness is broken, when we awake it will remerge with ourselves. We've done experiments with people who say they've had these experiences."

"But what if it doesn't?"

"Why," Hatchett said, "I guess we'd be dead to all intents and purposes, just a vegetable without a brain."

Miss Wilson and Doug Scott arrived just after noon with a truck full of equipment. With Hatchett's help, they began setting it up in the garage. Ralston watched them without getting involved; he knew nothing of the highly technical connections which had to be made. It all seemed to be equipment which Hatchett and his assistants had used before.

"Sophisticated electroencephalographs," Hatchett said to Ralston's query. "Other machines will measure the rise in dermal temperatures, perspiration levels, various bodily changes which indicate that we are in a state of agitation. In other words, these machines should be able to tell when we are in danger by our recorded reactions."

"I hope so. Well, my only worry now is how to tell Carol that I'll be sleeping out here."

"Unless I miss my guess, it will only be for a few days."

"She'll probably want to come too."

"As I said, there's a cot here if she wants to, but you must remember this could be dangerous if we make a mistake and one of those things gets through to this world."

"I'm all too well aware of that."

"I'm pretty sure we'll be able to control it, but I can't be one hundred percent sure."

"How much do Wilson and Scott know?"

"Everything. I had to tell them."

"And they accepted it?"

"Oh, more or less. It's a bit fantastic unless you've lived through it like we have. But they're professionals. They'll do their job."

"And they understand the danger involved?"

"They always have. The nature of this work is that we might run into some unseen dangers someday, things we couldn't cope with."

They moved about while Hatchett showed Ralston each of the machines and explained their functions. When he was finished, they stepped out into the bright sunlight for a cigarette.

"I wonder still if it wouldn't be wiser to wait until we understand the whole book."

"We can't wait. We've gone too far for that. Even if we gave up the whole project, we're still likely to make the journey now. Better to do it under lab conditions. As to understanding the book, well, we don't know how much we have absorbed. It's subliminal but enough to activate the powers. How can we stop?"

"I guess you're right," Ralston said with resignation, but he was no less ill at ease. He could not refute the logic of the argument.

Amongst the equipment were several gadgets that Hatchett had developed over his long career, sensors which could record any change in the physical environment from temperature to static electricity—in fact anything that might indicate an abnormality. In earlier years, those abnormalities could have been ghosts, poltergeists, or any other unknown presence. Hopefully, they now would give warning if any presence started to form in the garage while Ralston and Hatchett were "away." At least, they had every bit of equipment which had been developed. Hatchett was satisfied that their warning system was as complete as possible.

The plan was, if they had had a restful night, to continue looking through the book during the days. Hatchett had told Ralston that understanding might come as much from "Faculty X" as a precise translation of the whole.

Faculty X, he explained, was a known phenomenon whereby a subject had a sudden flash of understanding or insight. It very often happened to creative people. Some thought it was a special occult power; others explained it more along normal lines of inspiration. But some cases had shown that it went beyond the normal and, certainly, both of them had already experienced the acquisition of understanding which could not be explained logically and the use of powers which they had not known they possessed. In Hatchett's view, full realization of the whole book might come the same way, and then spill over into the conscious when fully absorbed.

That afternoon, when Carol's car drove up, Ralston left the others to setting up the new equipment. He found Carol in the kitchen unloading the groceries.

"Steak all right?" she asked, exhibiting two large T-bones.

"Fine."

She broke the plastic sealing wrapper and put the steaks into the refrigerator, then started unloading the vegetables into the sink.

"Carol," he started hesitantly, "we've got to talk about something."

"Go on."

"Darling, I'm going to have to sleep in the garage for a couple of nights."

She turned to him, puzzled. "Why?"

"This is a little difficult to explain. Last night, that dream . . . well, it wasn't a dream. Something was here in the house."

She visibly blanched. "The smell."

"That's right."

"What are you trying to say, Cary?"

He explained their thesis as quickly as he could. At first,

she could not accept it. Then, as with other matters connected to the whole experiment, she gave a grudging acceptance to the whole idea. But her partial understanding gave way to apprehension and then her demand that they both give up the project before anything dreadful happened. Ralston explained Hatchett's theory.

"You mean it's too late?"

"Yes. And it's much safer to have these experiences under laboratory conditions."

"That's why you're sleeping in the garage?"

"They have brought in some new equipment. It means we can be brought back before anything happens to us . . . and brought back in time to prevent anything following us. Otherwise, Carol, anytime I fall asleep I could make that journey and it could be dangerous to both of us."

She thought for a long time before saying, "I want you to take all the safety precautions you can. But I want to sleep in the garage too."

"I wish you wouldn't. If we make a mistake and one of those things comes back with us . . ."

"I'll take that chance. Cary, if anything happened to you, I wouldn't want to live either."

"Don't talk like that."

"You're all I have. God, why didn't you stop when I asked you, before it was too late?"

"That's spilt milk, Darling. Besides, even knowing what I do now, I'm not sure I could have given it up. I know that sounds selfish and I don't mean it to be. You know that I love you as much as any man could love a woman. I'd do anything for you. But even so I have to follow where events lead me just the same as if I were a test pilot or a soldier. Because this is dangerous doesn't mean I love you any the less. It's just something I have to do."

"Oh, Cary," she said, flinging her arms around his neck and burying her face in his chest. "I'm afraid."

He hushed her. "Hatchett knows what he is doing. Every precaution is being taken."

"Then I'll sleep in the garage with you."

"Darling."

"I'll sleep in the garage," she said with finality.

Knowing that further argument was futile, he agreed with a sigh.

She kept her arms around his neck for a long time, clinging hard, and he felt a lump in his throat. Carol's love for him had been the one real thing in the world, the only thing that really mattered to him, and yet he had risked it all on this venture and it made him feel very guilty. Few people had the kind of love they had. It was not always stated or even demonstrated but it was as real as the house, the garden, or the sky above. Now it was too late to stop the chain reaction of events. He had passed the point of no return, and there was no profit in complaining about having gone into it in the first place. Accepting Hatchett's logic, he knew that he would have to finish the job now or never be safe. There was no other answer. But if something did happen to him, what would happen to Carol? Oh, yes, people go on, but a wound the size of this one could never completely heal. They were like one person.

Saddened, Ralston accepted her condition that she be with him at night, though he knew his spirit might be millions of light years away, and that one morning she might awake to find nothing left of him but the husk of a man who no longer was. At worst, she might be facing a monster of indescribable terror and a hideous death. And still there was nothing he could do to alter it. If they had to face danger, it was better to do so while Mary Beth Wilson and Doug Scott were on guard with their electronic sentries than some night when he and Carol were alone . . . some night perhaps years away, when his subconscious once more activated the hidden power.

He kissed her with more feeling than he had ever known.

That evening, around eleven, the Ralstons made their way to the garage. It was a clear night, cold, and the stars glittered above. Cary looked up at them for a long time, wondering where he would be later that night. It was an eerie and remote feeling. Hatchett was quite cheery and confident when they arrived.

"I hope you'll be comfortable," he said to Carol. "We've put your cot next to Cary's. Just think of it as though we were on a safari," he said lightly.

She found it difficult not to respond in kind, despite her fear. "I'll be perfectly all right."

He turned to Ralston. "If you're ready, we can start wiring you up."

Scott approached Ralston and the latter lay down on his cot. The assistant then put various bands around his wrists and ankles, and a much wider leather band with metallic contacts around his chest. Other devices were attached to the surface of his skin at points on his thighs, upper arms, and fingers. From all of this apparatus, wires ran back to machines, which in turn were connected with a small, portable computer that continually spewed printouts. Miss Wilson checked the information as it was produced. Finally, a wide band with several antennae, each with wires, was put around his head. Encumbered though he was, Ralston was not uncomfortable.

"Don't worry about turning over," Scott said. "The wires and attachments are strong enough. Besides, Mary Beth and I will be watching all night."

Reassured somewhat, Ralston nodded. He glanced over to Carol, who regarded him with some amusement. His ridiculous appearance at least had dissipated her fears. He kissed her.

"I feel like the Bride of Frankenstein."

"Just go to sleep," he said with mock severity.

She rolled over and closed her eyes. Ralston lay there while Scott finished wiring Hatchett.

"Everything reads normally," Miss Wilson said.

"Good," Hatchett replied. "Now remember, use any means to wake us, including electric shock."

"Don't worry, Doctor," Scott said, with that kind of smooth assurance that airline captains are famous for, "we've got it all under control."

Nonetheless, it made Ralston feel better about things. He had confidence in Scott and Mary Beth. He knew that everything humanly possible was being done. That was all one could ask. Still, sleep did not come easily. He was not in the familiar surroundings of his own bedroom. There were strangers sleeping in the same room and the whirr of machinery. And memories of the previous night were not easily avoided. He stared up at the beams along the ceiling and listened to Carol's easy, even breathing next to him. Her presence was at the same time comforting and disturbing—he was worried about her but he needed her. After some time, the strain of the day pushed him into an uneasy slumber.

In the semidarkness, Mary Beth and Scott kept their eyes glued to the printouts from the computer and moved silently among the other machines, checking, watching, guarding. The needles zigzagged steadily across the charts showing all was regular. The two assistants sipped coffee from thermos bottles. Even though they had slept during the afternoon, the long night's vigil was tedious and they both hoped their concentration would not stray. Even though they found it difficult to totally accept Hatchett's explanation, they respected and trusted him. The hours passed; respiration, brain waves, dermal electricity, perspiration levels, and various other bodily functions were recorded and the information put through the computer. Minutes ticked by slowly. A dog barked in the distance. The night was still.

Ralston felt himself drifting up and through the roof, gathering speed, rushing out again into the chasms of space through the empty reaches of the Milky Way and beyond, past the whole network of light which was the cluster of galaxies that made up their universe, through the enormous void past other universes and supergalaxies until he was standing once more in the crazy-quilted jungle at the other end of the corridor of time. Hatchett was ahead, pushing through the bright-colored foliage, moving with the same slow-motion floating movements as himself. In the distance they could hear the ominous slobbering grunts and the heavy crashing of gigantic things coming through the trees behind them. Still they pushed forward with silent determination until they emerged from the heavy growths and found themselves looking down into a vast purple plain, across the face of which sparkled a million lights. Beyond the plain, in the distance against the orange sky, they saw the opalescent green towers reaching up, shimmering and translucent. The plain beckoned to them and drew them toward it, emanating a mesmerizing radiance. They floated down the slopes and started across the plain, drifting like underwater swimmers. On and on they went until they could see small hills on their left where gases seeped up from bubbling potholes of boiling slime. Slithering out of one was a great gray mass of loathsome horror. They moved as fast as they could. Then something reared up before them, a great birdlike reptilian form hovering, reddened eyes staring hotly, and the horrid beak salivating a dark fluid, which dribbled down its front. At the end of the leathery wings were cruel tridactyl claws. The thing moved along on hundreds of tiny snakelike legs which seemed incapable of supporting it. It pressed toward them with surprising speed. Ralston was transfixed with terror as the thing came for him, and behind it, other disgusting forms were moving, liverish jellyfish, oozing octopodidae, crawling masses of unrecognizable form, a motley of demons to join in the feast.

Hatchett snatched him back and he recovered his resolve. They would have to retreat from their goal. They saw a dark cave in a small hill near them and ran into it. The things did not follow but moved silently into positions before the cave. They had only one line of movement, back into the pitch blackness. From the depths of the dismal caverns came nauseating odors. Still they pressed on, down, down, deeper into the blackness and heat. There was a gabble of sounds around them and shining eyes seemed to follow them. Down into the measureless depths, through dank grottoes of slime and putrefaction, they floated in their half-movements. Some irresistible horror was drawing them to its bosom and they could not go back. Cracks of molten rock glowed, spewing down the walls, and choking vapors engulfed them, coming up from the ground. The heat was dizzying. Streams of lava poured by them and behind the rocks dark shapes darted to and fro and yet, though seized by terror, they could but go on down until in the very pit of the awful place, they were confronted by the numbing horror of the great pulsating creature, its tentacles flailing out toward them while behind them a jabber of horrid unseen shapes closed the circle.

Ralston's face stung sharply and then felt wet. He was sucked into a whirlpool of colors and in the midst of the maelstrom he heard Carol's voice calling out to him, and in a compaction of time, he saw the blur of the limitless voids and felt a slap on his face and opened his eyes to see Carol against the backdrop of the garage. He retreated through the eons in an instant and reentered himself. He came awake with a start and pushed himself up. Hatchett too was springing to his feet, tearing off the equipment which encumbered him. Ralston did the same.

"There's something forming in the corner," Mary Beth said, with breathless shock.

"Concentrate, Cary," Hatchett demanded.

The two men turned toward the corner and used all their strength to block the formation. Carol and the two assistants could see the formless dots whirling and heard the sounds and smelled the breath of hell. The buzzing and whirring increased and then stopped. There was nothing in the corner.

"It's all right," Mary Beth said, back at the computer.

Hatchett sagged into a chair. Carol was still pressed back against the garage wall, wide-eyed. It took some time before all of them could react normally again. Hatchett went over to the machines and looked through the printouts. Ralston held Carol, who asked no questions and wanted no answers.

"There's no doubt," Hatchett said, holding a stack of printouts. "We *were* there. Something left our bodies, something undefinable for the machines, but we know. We *were* there."

"Then it exists," Ralston said incredulously. "But where?"

"So far that we have no numbers to express it. So far."

They gave Carol a sedative but she did not sleep. She just watched and listened through a numbness caused by the drug and the aftermath of her fright.

"We stopped them. Yes, Cary, we stopped them."

"But it almost got us."

"Each time we grow stronger." Hatchett pondered, "We could have been anywhere. We could have traveled beyond time and space, past or future, or through some fourth dimension. But next time we will reach that city. That's where we'll find the secrets unraveled. Through the portals of that city, Cary. Think of it."

CHAPTER TWELVE

◎

Half an hour later, Ralston had calmed Carol down as much as could be expected in the circumstances. The accumulation of incidents was shattering her normal composure. It was all beyond her belief, yet the manifestations were frightening her badly. Still, Carol had reserves of strength that could be called upon even in the face of the unseen terrors that lurked around them, and she knew that hysterics would only inhibit the solution of the problems. So slowly, she reached down inside herself for the resolve to help and not hinder. It was a monumental effort but she managed to swallow her fears enough to allow Ralston a chance to go over matters with Dr. Hatchett.

Hatchett, in the meantime, had been reading the printouts with his assistants. They had reached no new conclusions. There were not yet sufficient data on which they could form any solid theory and all they could do was continue to accumulate as much information as possible. Body functions had been normal until the moments of acute danger so at least there was some signal which could operate as a warning.

"But what if it's *not* real?" Ralston asked.

"How do you mean that?"

"I mean, what if it's all a figment of our imagination."

"That's possible, of course . . ."

"We've planted these ideas in our minds. We have, or the book has."

"That comes close to attributing powers to the book by itself. And if you do that, you are coming close to giving it magical powers. I don't see why you find that more logical than astral projection taking us to a real place."

"All right. The place itself is illogical. There's an ultra-modern city and yet, right alongside, you have those prehistoric monsters. A race superior enough to build such a city would certainly have eliminated the monsters long before. How much wildlife of any sort is there around any modern city on Earth?"

Hatchett shrugged inconclusively.

"Another thing, if you really think about it, that underworld is pretty close to ideas of Hell."

"That crossed my mind too."

"So you see, it could well be a figment of our imagination. Or to carry on with your own theory, suppose that's our immemorial memory bringing up a picture of primeval life?"

"There were never such creatures on Earth."

"That we know of," Ralston said. "But even immemorial memory could play tricks, couldn't it? You know how our own normal memory can distort things after a long time."

"I can't deny the possibility."

"And this is also the product of *two* minds. Your memory or imagination mixed with mine so it comes out something that exists in neither alone."

"But the thing followed us back."

"PK again. If PK can create an unseen force to lift a table, why not a *visible* apparition . . . or even a smell?"

Hatchett sighed with frustration and disillusionment.

Scott, who had been listening, stepped toward them. "I hate to disagree with you, Professor, but I think he's got a valid argument."

Carol was heartened by Ralston's conjecture.

"I quite understand, Doug," Hatchett said. "I have no real evidence, just a hunch. And Cary, of course you may be right. As far as we understand things at the moment, within the limits of what we understand not only about the book but about parapsychology, it's as logical an explanation as any. But it doesn't answer everything. For example, who wrote the book? Where did that knowledge come from?"

Ralston hesitated and Scott looked bemused. "We talked about there being an ancient race on Earth," Ralston said. "Mu or Atlantis."

"That's more difficult for me to accept than something from outer space. Oh, there could have been a Lost Continent and there could have been an advanced race living on it, but *this* advanced? I don't think so. If they had progressed that far, they would have been all over the Earth, not just limited to one corner. Our civilization, which is *not* as advanced as the knowledge in that book, has spread itself to the four corners of the earth. Wouldn't that race have conquered and colonized just as we've done? Wouldn't they have nedeed minerals and resources just as we do? And yet, nowhere on earth is there any trace of them."

"We do have some comparative advances," Scott said, "as in Egypt and Peru."

"Certainly. And I could agree that there well might have been some connecting intelligence, but it's not the kind of knowledge that's reflected in the book. Cary, you understood a highly advanced theory of rocketry, which could only have come from the book. What other advanced knowledge is there we can't even prove because it goes beyond anything we understand today? In my mind, there's quite a difference between understanding rocketry and building a pyramid. That kind of knowledge needs a highly technical establishment . . . factories, laboratories, practical technology. But there isn't the least trace of anything like that anywhere on Earth. So I discount the possibility that an ancient race could have marshaled the science as set forth in the book."

"All right," Ralston said. "I'll even go along with UFOs or Flying Saucers. You and I talked about various possible sightings. But those were material, corporeal beings who traveled in space vehicles. What you're talking about with astral projection is something else. Besides, if those people had the ability to travel by astral projection, who came in the spaceships?"

Hatchett threw up his hands to at once indicate concession to the point and lack of any cogent answer to counter it.

"You can't even say it developed later," Ralston added for emphasis, "because if, as you say, man is a descendant of those space people, this ability in you and me to travel by astral projection is a throwback to them. They would have had it too."

"Astral projection has its limitations, Cary. *We* can only do it when we're asleep. When our bodies wake, we have to return. The Ka cannot exist without the body."

"Even if astral projection was proven, the world we visit might not exist. It could be in the past. If our Ka is traveling faster than the speed of light, back along the curve of space, then according to the theory of relativity we would be going back in time. Or for that matter, it could be something in the future, perhaps even right here on Earth. It could be two million years ago on Earth or two million years from now."

"Yes," Hatchett agreed, "and it could be in an entirely different dimension coexisting in the same spatial plane as Earth. But for the moment, let's assume it does exist and that once it was inhabited by beings who had the same ability to travel by astral projection as we do. Let's also assume that it exists billions and billions of light-years from us. So, if the speed of light were a constant, and no matter could pass through it, they would be unable to make the journey to earth because it would take billions and billions of years at sub–speed-of-light velocity."

"Suppose they could live that long?" Scott interjected. "There are theories that life could be prolonged almost indefinitely by replacing parts and so forth."

"Even if they could live that long, the trip would be unbearable. But even if life were prolonged almost indefinitely, as you say, that's not forever. Then too, you have to remember that they would not come directly to Earth. They would have had to explore millions of other worlds. More time."

"Unless, as you say, they used astral projection," Ralston said.

"Right. They could explore that way, perhaps, but they could not colonize that way."

"Then why do they have to?" Scott asked.

"They could have used up their own natural resources. Eventually, we will on Earth, so we'll have to look elsewhere. They might even have used up what was available in their own sector of the universe. After all, we could be dealing with a race billions of years older than man. But a Ka cannot colonize and dig minerals. No, they would need a way to manifest their physical being here. Unless,"

Hatchett said brightening, "there was another base for the Ka."

"Another body?" Scott asked.

"An exact duplicate," Hatchett said with some assurance. "Yes, because the Ka could not merge with anything less than an exact duplicate. It wouldn't fit." He was still talking but thinking beyond.

"You mean they made a synthetic body?" Ralston scoffed. "Even so, how could they get it here?"

"Let me take those one at a time. We are doing experiments right now to create life in a laboratory. Once that hurdle is crossed, there is no theoretical reason why any type of life can't be produced. After all, a human is only a certain combination of chemicals and atoms. And as to your second question, they might be more willing to experiment with a duplicate. They could always replace it. For example, they might shoot a stream of atoms through space at greater than the speed of light to be reassembled in our solar system. Later the Ka joins it."

"What happens to the original?" Ralston asked.

"Some sort of suspended animation. They might freeze it and revive it when needed again. Yes, both the Ka and the stream of atoms could travel enormous distances in instants."

Ralston shook his head skeptically. "I don't know."

"You surely can't deny the possibility of life on other planets? The law of probability does not allow you to. And that life could be fifty thousand years behind us, or fifty thousand years ahead of us. Try to imagine where science will take us in fifty thousand years. You can't, no more than a caveman could imagine an Apollo mission to the moon."

"So then man would be the descendant of these spares?"

"Possibly," Hatchett said almost lightly.

"But we can't live almost indefinitely," Scott said.

"We don't know that they could either. We only used that for an assumption. However, the mutations may have been more fragile than the originals. Perhaps we weren't such perfect copies. Our original powers waned or were forgotten. In any case, we lost contact. Conditions on earth might have created a slightly different evolutionary progression. Their Kas would no longer fit. We went on our own merry way, developed another species, close to them but not exactly the same."

They all thought about this for a few minutes and then Ralston said, "But that's only another theory. It isn't any more conclusive than what I said."

"Admitted," Hatchett said.

"So that brings us back to square one. Well, maybe not. I don't know if I can make this clear but let's assume our Kas travel to this distant planet. We can see it but can it see us? We would be existing in another dimension, something nonmaterial."

"Yes," Hatchett said.

"Then how can those things attack us unless they are in the same dimension as we are? In other words, those monsters are some kind of Ka themselves."

"That's an interesting point." Hatchett was perturbed by the idea. "Unless the whole thing isn't real, as you say, but some kind of reflection."

"So we come back to my idea again."

Hatchett was tired. "I'll have to think about it some more. If only we had some positive little clue, something we could go on . . ."

"We could go back to the book," Ralston said.

"Maybe we should. We'll just keep looking at it even though we don't seem to understand and hope that Faculty X pushes us a little further. That's about all I can suggest right now. But we mustn't get too tired. Whatever it is, we are going to have the same experience when we sleep again. We'll need all our resources."

"It'll be dawn in about fifteen minutes," Ralston said. "Why don't we have some breakfast?"

They all agreed. They also agreed to drop the subject for a while and give their minds a rest.

None of them discussed the project again that day, but none of them could stop thinking about it. Ralston had to admit to himself that his imagination was not big enough to encompass the scope of their contemplations. The concept was so immense that it was beyond his grasp. Reality was mixed with unreality and he could not separate the one from the other and if he tried to press toward a conclusion, his mind rebelled and left him facing a blank. No matter which path of reasoning he tried, it always ended the same way.

In the afternoon, he looked through the book with Hatchett. They did not read closely but just scanned the pages, glancing over the still undecipherable symbols and words, hoping that by osmosis or Faculty X some tiny glimmer of understanding might register. But at the end of the day there were no revelations, no new comprehension, just the same mind-boggling confusion.

Ralston took Carol to the movies that night. Neither of them was wholly able to concentrate on the comedy but it served to relax them just a little and when they returned home, they were a tiny bit more willing to face the night. Once again the two men were wired up to the machines; Mary Beth and Doug monitored the dials, while Carol looked on apprehensively from her cot next to her husband. None of them slept for a long time. Hatchett had ruled out the use of drugs for fear that it might delay their awakening too long or that it could dull their mental prowess. Anxiety, however, could not hold off exhaustion and soon they were all sleeping deeply.

For the third night running, Hatchett and Ralston found themselves on the strange other world. They were not in the same place and they were even closer to the city than before, near enough to see that the towers were of many colors, not only the emerald green they had seen before, but a myriad of ruby reds, umbers, and deep purples, and the textures seemed also to be of jewel-like substance. It was such a beautiful sight that both could only stand and gape for some time before trying to move toward it. On various levels, bridges connected the buildings, and along them whizzed conveyances of some type. What had looked static and quiet from afar now revealed itself to be a bee-hive of activity. Inside that city were the beings they had come to see. The rows of towers stretched back until they diminished into the horizon; a complex of buildings, so great that neither could imagine its size, and surround-ing it all was a high wall of the shimmering, translucent green material. The closer they moved, the more they realized that the towers reached up for miles into the sky and the more awed they were by the wondrous spectacle before them.

It was difficult to move. Everything was heavy all around them; the air viscous and thick. They had to fight hard to progress but the fabulous city beckoned them on, and on they went, each step taking them closer to the answers they sought and perhaps the beginning of a whole new age for man. They swam against the air, dragging up each foot to follow the next, reaching almost as if to claw at the atmosphere for handholds.

Suddenly the monster reared up in front of them so quickly that they could not avoid it. It blocked their way with its heart-chilling terror. They could not step aside in time and there was no cover to protect them and this time they were determined not to retreat into what could be a final trap. They had not time to set their minds against the red-eyed monstrosity with its ugly tridactyl claws, nor could they avoid the heavy stench that emanated from it. Hatchett backed away and tripped and in an instant the thing had slashed out, ripping open his calf. Ralston pulled Hatchett back. The thing hovered directly over them and was coming down.

"You're hurt," Scott said, shaking Hatchett awake. Ralston sat bolt upright in bed. Carol too was awake. Hatchett's leg was gushing blood. For a moment, Ralston could not acclimate himself to the state of wakefulness and the transfer of what had happened in the dream to what was in front of him now. Hatchett was bleeding! The wound was just as it had been in the dream. Hatchett himself seemed in a state of shock and then reached down and clamped his hands around his leg. Scott had taken off his belt and had wrapped it around Hatchett's leg as a tourniquet.

Carol, with characteristic coolness when faced with a real problem, was on her feet. "I'll get some bandages," she said, and headed for the door.

Hatchett fell back in pain. Ralston got himself together to assist. Mary Beth wet a handkerchief from the garden hose and began to daub gently around the wound. In a few moments, the flow of blood was stanched. Carol came back in with the first aid kit and the two women cleansed and bandaged the wound. Though it appeared not too deep, they decided to ask Dr. Braine to come over just in case.

"You'd better take me up to the house," Hatchett said

when his color came back. "It wouldn't do for the doctor to see all this," he said, waving a hand toward the equipment.

"I guess you're right. Give me a hand, Scott, will you?"

Scott and Ralston made a cradle with their hands and carried Hatchett into the study. Ralston gave him a drink of whisky.

"Well, Cary," Hatchett said tightly, "do you still think it's a figment of our imagination?"

"I don't know what to think."

"I suppose you're thinking that this could have been psychosomatic?"

"You're in no shape to go into that now . . ."

"I'd rather talk. Well, is that what you're thinking?"

"It's not impossible."

"Scott?" Hatchett said, looking toward his assistant.

"I don't know what happened, but it is possible, Doctor. You remember those experiments under hypnosis with the ice cube."

"What's that?" Ralston asked.

"When the subject was under hypnosis," Hatchett said, "they put an ice cube against his arm and told him it was a red-hot poker. A wound such as would be caused by a hot poker appeared on the subject's arm."

"Well . . ." Ralston said with a wide sweep of his arms.

"Well, dammit, I *know* I'm right about this," Hatchett said with determination. "That book was meant to give us a way to reach that place. There's no other explanation for it."

"But there's no way we can prove it, not even to ourselves."

"Short of bringing back soil samples the next time, I don't see how we can," Hatchett said sardonically. "We've got two possible theories and I admit you have more scientific basis than I have but dammit, I've got a strong feeling about this. I just know it's got to be right."

"There is one thing that happened," Scott said in the pause.

"What?" Hatchett said, mildly interested.

"Well, when we saw the readings, I was coming to wake you both up, but then we saw the blood. I guess we both rushed to you. But Mr. Ralston, you woke up anyway before we got there."

Hatchett snapped his head toward Ralston. "You woke yourself up!" He clapped his hands joyfully. "Cary, you're getting control. Everytime we get a little more control."

"And every time it gets a little more dangerous," Ralston said.

"But there's no way to turn back."

"I wish there was."

"But there isn't," Hatchett insisted. "Don't allow yourself vain hopes. We have to concentrate. If we were shipwrecked, we'd have to gather food and build a shelter. It wouldn't do much good to sit on the beach looking for a ship."

"Oh, I know you're right, Doctor, but I can't help wishing it was different. We had a close call tonight."

"And something else happened too. You remember you wondered how those things could attack our Kas unless they were also of the same quality? But that attack also affected my physical body. It attacked my Ka but injured my body."

Just at that moment Dr. Braine arrived. "Hello, Cary," he said coming in.

"It's this gentleman," Carol said, leading him toward Hatchett. She introduced them all hurriedly.

"What are you all doing at five-thirty in the morning?"

Braine said, mostly to make conversation, while snipping off the bandage.

Everyone else exchanged glances. "Walking in the garden," Ralston said foolishly. "Dr. Hatchett tripped over a rake."

"I'd better give you a tetanus shot," Braine said. "Are you a medical doctor?"

"Ph.D." Hatchett said.

"Oh, what's your field?" He applied an antiseptic to the wound. "Do you want to roll up your sleeve?"

"I don't think your tetanus shot will have any effect on *these* germs," Hatchett said, but rolled up his sleeve.

"You never know." Braine administered the shot and rebandaged the wound. "You girls did a nice job. I don't think it will give you any trouble, but I'd stay off it for a day or two."

Hatchett nodded grumpily. "Thank you."

After the doctor left, Carol came back into the study and sat down. "I think I ought to tell you all something. I knew Cary was in danger."

"You what?" Ralston said.

"I knew you were in danger." She spoke quite calmly. "I don't know how I knew, I just knew."

"Mrs. Ralston," Hatchett said with incisive interest, "have you ever had ESP experiences before?"

"No."

"No matter. We all have the ability. Don't you see, Cary? Not only are you getting control, your signals are becoming more powerful. Your wife can pick them up. We are making progress. Don't doubt that for a minute. Every time, the power is growing."

"I don't know if I want her to see more."

"She's another safety factor," Hatchett said firmly.

"If I can help, I don't care what I see," Carol said.

233

"You don't know."

"Darling, if I can help what difference does it make?"

Ralston went to the window and looked out. It was getting light. "Now we're dragging her into this," he said, turning once more to Hatchett.

"Don't jump to conclusions," Hatchett advised. "She may sense your danger but that's only because you are sending out signals strong enough to be picked up. We all have ESP abilities. In normal circumstances, your wife does not use them. But when there is an extraordinarily powerful transmission, she does pick it up. That does not mean she will develop any of the other techniques unless she studies the book as we have done. So if you're worried that she may come with us, forget it. It's not in the cards."

"How can you be so sure?" Ralston snapped.

"I've had some experience in the field," Hatchett retorted.

"Well . . ." Ralston said sourly.

"Forget it. I promise you though, there's nothing to worry about on that score. But your wife will be a second line of defense. She may sense something that the machines don't. Let's be thankful for anything that might help and protect us."

Carol seemed rather hurt by Ralston's attitude, as if he were rejecting her help, so he sat down alongside her. In a few moments, a smile crossed her face. "I do appreciate it, Sweet," Ralston said finally.

"Okay. Just don't worry about me, now."

"I'll try."

"And try to think positively," Hatchett added. "We're doing much better. In time, we'll beat this."

"If we have the time," Ralston said.

Carol went shopping about eleven o'clock and Ralston

went out to the garage, but Hatchett was feeling too tired to go over the book. They decided to wait until the afternoon. Ralston decided to take a swim. It was a warm, beautiful day, perfect for a relaxing dip, so he walked out to the cabana and changed. The water was luxuriously refreshing and as he swam up and back the whole problem of the book seemed to fade away. For a few moments he managed to put it out of his mind completely. He crawled out of the pool and lay under the hot sun to dry off.

In the market the melons looked good, so Carol took two and headed for the meat counter. As she walked along she saw nothing that struck her fancy so she rang for the butcher. "I'd like a whole fillet, please."

"Going to barbecue?" the butcher said. "It's going to be a good night for it."

"Yes."

He slapped a piece of meat on the cutting block and trimmed it down, then brought it to the window and exhibited it. "It's a nice piece."

"It looks very nice," she answered.

"Anything else?" When she didn't answer, he looked up. "Is there something wrong, ma'am?"

Carol's face was a mask of terror. Suddenly she turned and ran, leaving her groceries behind. She dashed through the line at the checking counter, pushing by people and paying no attention to the muttered protests of the jostled customers. She ran to the car, her heart bursting with anguish. Her hands were trembling so she could hardly get the key into the ignition. Then she wheeled the big car out of its parking slot, and lurched into the street. She drove in a frenzy, fearing that she would be too late.

After such a night, Ralston had found it impossible to keep from drowsing. He knew he shouldn't but he was too tired to fight it and if he could only have a few moments, it would be enough. The minute sleep came over him, he was speeding through the tunnels of time and found himself in front of the very walls of the city. The towers of the buildings loomed up over him in awesome grandeur. The conveyances flashed back and forth silently and he stepped up to the gates and looked in. The streets were empty! As far as he could see down the wide boulevards, there was nothing moving, no living thing, no vehicle; the city was deserted! Yet up above, on the bridges between the towering buildings, conveyances were crisscrossing at high speeds. He didn't understand. But he knew that the city was deserted. Before the shock of that discovery could wear off, he saw a solitary figure stagger out of one of the buildings. At first he couldn't believe his eyes but then he saw that the figure was Whitney! Ralston reeled with surprise. He tried to call out but the words would not come out of his mouth. Whitney! The figure stumbled along in a soporific state, then disappeared into another building. How had Whitney got there? Ralston could not understand what was happening.

Tentacles shot out around his throat and neck. He turned to see the awful, pulsating mass. He tore at the tentacles, which were pulling him toward the terrible mouth. One of them wrapped around his forehead and he felt his brain oozing away. Ralston concentrated with all his power but he could not fight off the thing. He knew that the end was inevitable and fear bunched up in his stomach as he struggled, while slowly, inexorably, the thing was drawing him closer.

Carol's car screeched to a halt at the garage and slammed into the wall. Carol jumped out screaming, "Cary! Cary!" Terror-stricken, she ran toward the pool.

Scott was the first out of the garage. Hatchett hobbled after him with Mary Beth's help. They all saw Carol running toward the swimming pool. Scott ran after her and Hatchett hopped along as fast as he could.

When he could see the pool, his blood ran cold. There was Ralston's body sleeping peacefully alongside the pool and, not more than fifty feet away, a titanic struggle was taking place. A huge elm was ripped from its bed and thrown fifty feet toward the house, almost knocking Carol down. She fell trying to avoid it. "Cary, Cary!" she screamed again, as she tried to crawl on her hands and knees toward him. Great chunks of turf spat up near to her as the lawn was ripped and torn. Scott ran up alongside but was knocked back by some invisible force and sprawled. He struggled to his feet and ran on. The grass between Scott and Carol and where Ralston was lying was chewed up, spattering in all directions, and they could not get across it.

Hatchett put his whole mind to extreme effort of will. He could feel his brain throb painfully but he concentrated every ounce of his energy. The storm between Ralston and Carol and Scott became more violent and they were being tossed about in the energy waves. The pain in Hatchett's leg was handicapping his concentration. He had to eliminate it. He had to put pain out of his mind and focus on that psychostorm. His face was contorted with agony as he pushed himself to the limit.

Despite Scott's trying to hold her back, Carol got to her feet and dashed through to Ralston, falling on top of him. The waters of the pool leaped up over them, drenching them. Carol dragged Ralston back from the edge as the whole pool lifted up en masse and jackknifed.

Hatchett collapsed.

When he came to, they were all sitting stunned on the ruins of the lawn. Carol was holding Ralston's head close to her breast. Scott was gasping like an athlete who'd just

237

finished a race. Mary Beth was in some kind of shock. Hatchett pulled himsef up and limped toward Ralston and Carol.

With a deep breath, Ralston looked up, "I'm all right."

Carol was still shaking and Hatchett leaned down to her. "Are *you?*"

She looked at him blankly.

"Thanks to you, we're all all right," Hatchett said.

It took them several minutes before they could straggle back into the garage and sit down. All of them had been severely shaken but none was really hurt. After a time, Ralston said, "I fell asleep."

"I never should have let you out of my sight," Hatchett said. "From now on, we've all got to stay close by."

"I won't leave the house," Carol said.

"I got to the city," Ralston said.

"We can talk about that when you feel up to it."

"I'm all right. We haven't time to waste, Doctor."

Carol nodded at Ralston. "Go on."

"I got to the city, right up to the gates. But it's deserted."

"We saw those cars . . ." Hatchett said.

"They must be automatic. The streets are deserted . . . except . . ." he cocked his head as he remembered, ". . . except for Professor Whitney."

"Whitney?"

"The professor who went insane."

"You *saw* him?"

"He was wandering as if he didn't know where he was going . . ."

"He was inside?"

"Yes."

"He made it. But why him?"

"And he's insane," Ralston said.

"Oh, God," Carol moaned.

"Why is he there?" Hatchett pounded the desk. "Why is Whitney there?" he said with more force.

"His Ka is stranded, isn't it?" Ralston said.

"Perhaps." Hatchett pondered a few seconds. "Of course, he didn't know what he was doing. He was groping, following Nelson's notes, but Nelson didn't know what he was doing either. Yes, that must be it. Whitney is lost. He doesn't know where he is. He doesn't know how he got there. He doesn't know how to get back either. And the whole thing must be pretty shattering to him. But why is the city deserted? If there's nothing there for us . . ."

"I didn't see anyone except Whitney."

"There's a reason. There has to be a reason. Why would They abandon the city?"

"They could have died out."

"Then it's all for nothing? Is that what Whitney discovered?" The thought demoralized Hatchett and his head sagged onto his chest. He stared down at the floor for a long time. "No!" he said, his head snapping upright again. "I can't accept that. There's got to be a purpose behind it all. Our efforts will not be in vain. There's an answer and we're going to find it!"

The others were no longer convinced of that, certainly not Ralston. The critical question was whether Whitney had sought and attained their goal only to find it was an empty illusion. His Ka was in limbo with no place to go, stranded in a voided dream. Or it could be what Ralston had thought all along, a figment of their imaginations, translated into PK power through ESP.

After lunch, Ralston tried to remember what had happened at the end, when he was being drawn toward the pulpous gray mass, but the struggle had been so disjointed and out of focus that he could remember but little, except the cataclysmic battle to save himself from a ghastly death. He shuddered. It had ended in a confusion of jumbled images; Carol's body tumbling onto his and the pool water crashing down over them both. All these thoughts ran through his mind as he walked around the pool to survey the damage. It looked as though some giant hand had ripped it from its moorings and broken it in the middle. It rested lopsided like an inverted V near the hole that had been its anchorage. In the garden around it, there were huge gaping holes in the lawn and a large cavity where the elm had been. The tree now lay on its side, its fingerlike roots reaching forlornly into the air. The aftermath bore mute witness to the fury of the cosmic storm.

While Carol prepared dinner, Hatchett and Ralston sat out on the patio under a brilliant vault of stars. The winds from the desert rustled the trees. Looking up at the sky, Ralston had a hollow feeling in his stomach. It might be that this night would prove crucial, and both he and Hatchett were all too aware of what might lie ahead of them, a terrible fate at the mercy of the beasts or the just as disquieting possibility that there was nothing at the end of the trail.

"We have to concentrate on getting into the city," Hatchett said. "This afternoon, you did land at the very gates. That's where we must go tonight, and then, straight into that city without delay. It has to be tonight because the strain is telling on both of us. We can't go on indefinitely." Hatchett's face was momentarily lit by the glow of his cigarette.

"I've wondered," he went on. "What happens to the Ka if the body dies? With Whitney's Ka up there, what is left of him on earth is a mere shell. The psychiatrists call it catatonia but we know it's something far different. But if the body dies, does the Ka wander on, a form without hopes of ever finding another base? Does that explain ghosts? Can the Ka marshal enough power once in a while to materialize? Take our monsters, for example. Is there a brief flowering of energy to manifest them on earth?"

"I wonder if Nelson or the baron got as far as that world," Ralston said almost wistfully.

"Unless they were unknowing conduits. Those things might have appeared on their doorsteps before they understood enough . . . And have you thought, those monsters attack the Ka, Cary? An injury to the Ka also destroys the material body. My leg," he offered as an example.

"Then the Ka is destructible?"

"It would appear so. But it might not always be destroyed, as take Whitney for example."

"That only tells us that it is alive as long as the body lives. If the body dies, it could die too, if it is mortal. It dies or wanders."

"Or reenters," Hatchett said. "Do we know that the Ka cannot reenter a human form—not a fully developed one because there cannot be room for two Kas in one human, but in a baby perhaps, before the newly born Ka is sufficiently developed."

"That sounds very much like reincarnation."

"Close to it," Hatchett said matter-of-factly. "I wonder though if the Ka loses its identity when it merges with the new form. It may take on characteristics of the child and that could be the reason why our super-race could reenter humans. We might have changed . . . or they might have changed. Evolution can work in both camps."

"Have you got some idea?" Ralston asked.

"Just musing. But why speculate when tonight we may have the answers?"

The conversation drifted off at that point as both of them thought of the night's journey again. Though he desperately wished he could stop it, Ralston knew he could not. Even a nap by the pool had been enough to send him hurtling through the heavens again. There was little doubt that he would go again that night and that Hatchett would be with him. Ralston had barely escaped that afternoon, Hatchett the night before—would they be so lucky again?

After dinner, Ralston and Carol went to another movie while Hatchett went to the Music Center to listen to a Bach concert. Mary Beth and Scott were asleep upstairs, as they had been since two that afternoon. All would be in readiness at eleven o'clock sharp.

They were looking down at a planet as large as Earth's orbit around the Sun. In the far distance they could see the dim "white dwarf" sputtering out the end of its life, dwindling to a gaseous haze. Below them was a dead world, cold and dreary. How long had their sun been dying?

They drifted across the enormous face of the planet. There were other cities below them, not unlike the one they sought, but less impressive somehow. And then they were over their goal. From the ground, they had miscalculated its size greatly because it was as vast in area as the Pacific Ocean on Earth and the towers reached miles into the skies. They concentrated their energies on reaching it. They skimmed over the crazy-quilt jungle, across the purple plains, past the potholes boiling and steaming, then settled before the massive gates of the forbidden city.

They entered immediately and stood just inside, marveling at the towers, the swift and silent conveyances crisscrossing the elevated tramways above them, level after level, and the shimmering beauty of the buildings of ruby, emerald and sapphire. They stood spellbound and reverent before the rarefied symmetry and sublime purity of the sight before them.

The snorting made them turn. The thing was just outside the gates, its tentacles railing at the skies, but it did not follow. They were safe—at least from what lay outside the gates; but what lay ahead they had yet to face.

They started along the deserted streets that stretched ahead of them for miles upon miles, straight and broad, past the thrusting jeweled towers and by the wide and lush parks, but they encountered not one sign of life. Above them, on a thousand levels, the conveyances whisked along, stopped, then moved again. Yet even on the levels directly above them, they could see no living beings. The city lived on its own, running smoothly until eternity, but the architects of the overwhelming metropolis were gone—the city sailed on under its own power like a ghost ship.

They stepped into an amber building, into the colossal entrance foyer, and stared up toward the ceiling, which was out of sight. But as big as the building was, the doorways were only slightly larger than those on earth—large enough, they calculated, to accommodate a twelve-foot being. On one side, banks of translucent elevators shot up to the unseen stories above, traveling in no evident shaft, but on precise lines nevertheless. They stepped into one and were flashed upward in seconds at tremendous speed—floor after floor of fabulous sights flashed by, but there were no beings, only the machines of jeweled substance which continued their functions.

When the elevator stopped, they got out and walked until they exited from the building on one of the upper levels. Miles below them they could see the ground level they had left and miles above them the towers stretched out of sight. Around them wheels and cogs, levers and computers functioned silently, and components they could not understand, diaphanous shapes and colors that merged

243

and faded in mesmeric undulations. The breathtaking splendor around them had an obsessive allure they could not resist.

One of the conveyances was nearby and they stepped into it. It sped off between the towers, through canyons of jeweled substance, over the streets far below until they could see the most massive and fabulous building of them all before them, a great golden tower with flecked silver filigrees of such infinite beauty that both men were stunned. They stepped out of the conveyance and moved along the level into the fantastic foyer. Below them, atomic fires waxed and waned with rhythmic incandescence and in the center of the building was a great globe of monumental size, reflecting like a mirror and studded with diamonds, sparkling and dazzling their eyes and pulling them toward it. They moved as if in a trance, unable to resist its powerful attraction, and passed into the womb of it, where the glory of a million auroras burst about them. Particles of light flashed and darted about them and they were as if suspended in a crackling explosion of light.

And they knew.

The dying star and the search for new ways. Ka travel. The colonies and the quest for nonmaterial existence that would free them forever from the necessities of the tangible universe. But having sprung from the soil, they had first to purify the Ka, to remove the id and leave it behind, for only the cleansed ego could pass beyond the barriers and once it was done, they could not turn back, not even to rescue the Descendants, for if they crossed over into the same dimension as their id, the magnetic force to remerge would be irresistible. Reunited with their ids, they could never return. It was for the Descendants to find the path themselves and they had but one chance more. The Ancestors would send no more to them.

And the portals parted. Through the widening breach in the coruscating cyclorama, the finite destiny lay on the other side of time and space and the Earthlings looked upon perfection.

Carol was awakened by the muttered, urgent conversation between Mary Beth and Doug Scott. She came awake with a start. The moment she opened her eyes, Mary Beth turned toward her, on the verge of tears. Carol sprang past her to Ralston's side. There was a peaceful, beatific expression on his face. There were no wounds, no terror, but he was dead. There was no question but that both he and Hatchett were dead.

Carol burst into tears. Mary Beth put her arm around Carol's shoulders to comfort her, fighting off her own tears. "You should go back to the house."

"No!" Carol sobbed. "What happened?" she gasped in tear-choked words. "They were not in danger!"

"They just . . . stopped," a baffled Scott said. "Everything was normal. They were not afraid, no, it was more like contentment. And then, without any warning, everything stopped registering."

"Are you sure?" Carol sobbed, hugging the lifeless form of her husband.

Scott picked up Hatchett's wrist, then leaned his ear against the doctor's chest. "Yes, but you ought to call that doctor to make certain."

The tiny flicker of hope gave Carol strength. She dashed to the house to telephone Dr. Braine. He came immediately and went out to the garage. It took only a brief examination to confirm Scott's conclusion. Cary Ralston and Dr. Hatchett were both dead.

245

Dr. Braine came up to Carol tenderly, "Carol, I'm sorry, but he's gone. Both of them. I won't be able to tell you what happened until the autopsy."

Carol stiffened with repulsion. "No."

"In cases of mysterious death like this, there must be one."

"No," she said.

"All right," the doctor conceded, "we'll leave it until the morning. Shall I make the arrangements?"

"Arrangements?" she said with a dazed expression.

"They can't stay here," he said softly. Since she didn't react he turned to Mary Beth. "I'll take care of it in the morning. In the meantime, I'll give her something. Let's get her to the bedroom."

Carol was too stunned to offer much resistance and they led her out of the garage and upstairs to her bedroom with no trouble. Dr. Braine administered a heavy sedative by injection and within moments, she dropped off into a deep slumber. The physician went downstairs where Mary Beth and Scott were waiting.

"I'd like to ask you some questions."

Doug and Mary Beth exchanged glances. "All right," Mary Beth said.

"Do you have any idea what happened?"

"Not really," Scott said evasively.

"Did they both die at the same instant?"

"As far as we know," Mary Beth said. "According to the instruments."

"What *are* those instruments?"

"Ordinary medical equipment with some variations for our field," she answered.

"What is your field?" Braine asked.

"Parapsychology," she said wtih a mixture of pride and exculpation.

Braine reeled as if he'd been struck in the face. "I see," he said tersely. For a moment they all stood motionless. "You know, this will have to be reported."

"Because of our field?" Scott asked with recrimination.

"Well, you have to admit it looks rather odd," Braine said honestly. "I don't know what Cary Ralston had to do with all this. But to protect his name, I can call a friend of his on the police force. A captain," he said, trying to remember. "Mexican name. Yes, Fernandez, that's it. Do you have any objection?" he said, picking up the study telephone.

"No, why should we?" Mary Beth said indignantly. But her askance look toward Doug betrayed that assurance. It was difficult enough to explain parapsychology to academics, but a policeman . . .

Until Fernandez arrived, they sat in tense truce speaking only a few terse words. The police captain's eyes were ringed with fatigue and the shock of what Dr. Braine had told him over the telephone. They all went out to the garage and Fernandez looked briefly at the two bodies.

"I don't know what they were doing out here," Dr. Braine said in a straitlaced tone.

"I do," the policeman said flatly.

"You do?" Mary Beth said, her mouth open in surprise.

A half-smile crossed Doug's face and Dr. Braine's forehead creased into many frowns.

"What was the time of death?" Fernandez said.

"About an hour ago," Scott replied.

"Both at the same time?"

"At the same instant. You can look at the machines . . ." Mary Beth said helpfully.

"Later," Fernandez snapped. "Where's Carol?"

"I've given her a sedative. Captain, don't you think

247

there's something very odd about two men dying at the very same instant, in these circumstances?"

Fernandez stared sardonically at Braine, "Yes, it's odd."

"You certainly don't seem very impressed."

"I'm more impressed than you imagine, Doctor. I think I can handle it from here. Why don't you get some sleep? I'll see you in the morning."

"Well, I . . ." Braine huffed, surprised at the abrupt dismissal.

"Be a good guy, will you?" Fernandez added. The tone was friendly enough but there was an implied threat behind it. He took the doctor by the elbow and escorted him to the garage door.

"Very well. I'll come back to see Carol in the morning," he said, as if it were his own decision.

"You do that," the police captain called after him, as Braine stepped out into the darkness. He went back and stared down at Ralston. At least he was in one piece. It was better than he expected. "Could there have been any crossed wires?"

"No. I checked it thoroughly," Scott said.

"Okay, but we'll double check to make sure in the morning. You want to tell me?"

"What?" Mary Beth asked.

"What was going on."

"It's a bit difficult," she stammered, looking to Scott for help.

"I know about the book," Fernandez said.

Scott explained it quickly. It sounded even more fantastic than before.

"You believe all this?" Fernandez said.

"I had a great deal of respect for Dr. Hatchett . . ."

"I asked if you *believed* all this."

"Well, some of it was a little hard to swallow . . ."

248

"That's putting it mildly," Fernandez said with a grunt.

"Of course, I have some doubts . . ."

"Of course. Have you any idea what caused their deaths?"

"If you want my opinion . . ." Mary Beth volunteered.

"Sure."

"It's possible that they were both involved in a mutual fantasy which they shared through ESP. Psychosomatic causes may have brought on death. You know, it is possible for a man to *will* his own death. There are certain tribes in Central America . . ."

"Psychosomatic," Fernandez interrupted. "Not too bad. Listen to me, both of you," he said very seriously. "When I make my report we'll call your work *psychology*. Right?"

"Well, it is parapsychology," Miss Wilson corrected.

"Forget the 'para'. Just say psychology and leave it at that." He leveled his gaze on both of them.

"But people know what we do . . ." Scott said.

"Not out here. Just play this my way and the coroner won't give us any fuss. It won't even hit the local papers, let alone the national ones. Now, please, can we agree on that?"

Mary Beth and Doug looked rather relieved but somewhat puzzled. "If that makes you happier," Doug answered.

"It'll make us all happier and you know it. You don't want to try and explain this in court, do you?" Scott and Mary Beth shook their heads. Fernandez went on, "Well, I don't want to look silly either. There's a D.A. named Speke who might ask a lot of very embarrassing questions which we couldn't answer satisfactorily. And another thing, there's Carol to think of. It would make things difficult if her husband was a laughingstock."

"She knew all about the experiments."

249

Fernandez jumped to his feet. "Was she involved?" he asked urgently. Then without waiting for an answer he ran out of the garage and raced into the house. He took the stairs three at a time and threw open the door to the bedroom. He could see that nothing was wrong. Carol was sleeping peacefully so he went back downstairs. Mary Beth and Scott were waiting.

"Let's go into the study. I want all the details so we can work out our story. We've got to be clear on every detail and we haven't got much time."

As they disappeared into the study, Carol's eyes came open. The first streaks of light were coming through the window and pinioned in the light was Ralston. Carol scrambled out of bed and ran to him. "Cary," she said, throwing her arms around him. Over his shoulder, she could see Hatchett standing tranquilly.

"Carol, be calm," Ralston said softly.

"Cary . . ."

"You will understand soon." She looked up into his face and caught the glimpse of a rapturous glow. And she felt a power surging toward her from him.

"But . . . you were dead . . . Dr. Braine . . ."

"You will understand everything very soon," he said, again in the lulling, mellifluous tone. She knew that she would.

The study door opened and Mary Beth looked up, then half stood. With a gasp, she collapsed in a heap on the floor. Both Scott and Fernandez made a move toward her, but then snapped their attention toward the door. Fernandez' heart almost stopped. Scott stood trembling.

"Cary!" Fernandez uttered huskily, almost unable to form the word.

Ralston and Hatchett eased into the room gently. Carol

came in behind them as if sleepwalking. "You must not be afraid," Ralston said, in that soothing voice.

"Professor . . ." Scott gasped.

"Listen, Doug, you must listen," Hatchett said in a velvety quiet. Something about their voices seemed to calm Scott and Fernandez. "You will understand everything soon."

Ralston smiled warmly toward Fernandez. "You must correct the mistake Dr. Braine made."

"Mistake?" It was no mistake . . . but then he was looking at Ralston and Hatchett and they were not dead. "Yes, I will."

"You will be the first," Ralston said, indicating all of them. "You will understand, as we do, if you can. We can lead but we cannot make you follow."

"What are you talking about? Cary, are you all right?"

"I am better than I have ever been, Bob."

"But you were dead," Scott said finally.

"No," Hatchett countered, "you were mistaken. We were only away." The vibrance of his words waved over Scott. "Now we are here to help you, everyone. There is only one more chance."

"To do what?" Fernandez said rather breathlessly.

"To join Them. To know the Ultimate. To leave behind the beast. But it will depend which is stronger, the beast or the purified psyche."

"I wish I knew what you were talking about," the policeman said, in hopeless confusion.

"I don't mean to talk in riddles but there is much that you must understand. It will take time. We will need your help, all of you.

"This is the last time They will summon us. They will send no more messengers." Hatchett spoke quietly. "Yes, there have been messengers before, but sometimes even

251

they could not understand what was asked of them, nor why the id and the Ka must be separated to achieve the Ultimate. You see, the book has been on earth for thousands of years. If you think, you will know the messengers."

"What remains here will be the residue. What goes on will be the pure species." Ralston turned toward Carol and put his arms around her, kissing her gently.

"I believe in you, Darling." Tears of joy rolled down her face.

Fernandez stood without moving. It was all beyond him but somehow he trusted Ralston in spite of it.

Hatchett turned to Scott, "Let's put Mary Beth on the sofa."

"Yes," Scott said hurriedly, and before Hatchett could lift her the easy way, with his mind, Scott was struggling to get her up. Ralston and Hatchett smiled at each other. Scott would learn in time.

Some sixty miles away in Camarillo State Mental Hospital, Dr. Frankel was witnessing a miracle. He didn't believe in such things but there was no denying that Professor Whitney was normal, even though there was a peculiar aura of perfect peace around him. Frankel left the room, shaking his head in disbelief. When he put this into the *Psychiatric Journal,* they would be likely to come for him! Recovery from complete catatonia. Impossible, they would say. In any case, he would arrange for Whitney's release as soon as he could obtain the proper papers.

As he walked down the polished corridors, he had a compelling urge to contact Captain Fernandez. He didn't know why he should but he knew he must. There was something about Whitney . . .